CROSS-
COUNTRY

BAROMETER RISING

TWO SOLITUDES

THE PRECIPICE

HUGH MacLENNAN

CROSS-COUNTRY

HURTIG
Publishers
EDMONTON

Published by Hurtig Publishers
by special arrangement with Wm. Collins Sons & Co.

© 1949 by Hugh MacLennan

International Standard Book No. 0-88830-058-1

First Hurtig edition published 1972

PRINTED IN JAPAN

TO MY MOTHER

INTRODUCTION TO THE
NEW EDITION

W HEN Mel Hurtig said he wished to reprint my first
book of incidental nonfiction, I would have thought
him crazy if I hadn't known that he wasn't. I doubt if I
opened this book more than five times between 1949 and
1970 and that, my friends, was a period aeons longer even
than the one between the fall of the Bastille and Waterloo.
During it the world's psyche went into such convulsions
that its present master can be neither the Pentagon nor
the Kremlin nor even the multinational corporation, but
some species of sphinx that has come back like a king to
earth and has been paying his subjects with a royal wage
I can't honestly believe that all of them deserve.

Before re-reading *Cross-Country* my recollections of its
contents were generally vague and were not pleasurable,
for this book was associated in my mind with that numbed
period when the joy of release from the Nazi horror was
obliterated almost instantly by what was done at Hiro-

shima, soon to be followed by the Cold War and the universal surrender to technology, Madison Avenue and international propaganda on a scale quite unparallelled. Anyone in those years who was not a socialist, a communist or a small-l liberal—I admit that these categories contained all but perhaps two percent of the intellectual population of the West—was driven to the fearful conclusion that man's real troubles are not caused by political and economic systems and only incidentally by scoundrels, but by the cruel contradictions planted in his nature by no less an authority than the God of Evolution Himself. Anyway, during those last years of the 1940s we were wheeled out of the OR of the Hot War into the recovery room of the Cold War and the Affluent Society, two words as inseparable as Siamese twins because in the American system the latter depended on the former. There we remained, our minds still doped by the anaesthetic and the sedatives, until the end of the 1950s.

In those days I was small-l liberal in what might vaguely be called my intellect, but I now recognize—and can call three novels as witnesses—that my intuitions were relaying to my intellect a set of signals my intellect was too intellectually respectable to decode. If anyone has read my novel *Each Man's Son,* which I began about the time I was finishing the last of these magazine pieces, he will know what I mean. Moreover, in these essays I was a guerrilla on alien territory and had to speak the language of its proprietors if I was to speak at all; in this case, the proprietors were magazine editors, as serious and full of uplift as Macaulay himself, the man who fathered the article and practically put the essay out to pasture. The editors used to call the stuff I sent them "think pieces" and I can truly say that they stretched to the absolute limit the amount of thoughtfulness any successful editor of the day was willing to print.

Editors, then as now, insisted that their writers be controversial and though styles in controversial topics change with the times, they seldom violate the basic principle that if you wish to be profitably controversial you should take on some lion or tiger who has lost his teeth and is too old and decrepit to defend himself. Twenty years ago the schools and the Protestant Churches were safe targets, though not the Catholic Church nor the Synagogue. About sex you could be coy or jocular, you could be highminded, you could argue that sex can be good for your health under proper conditions, but no matter what your *point d'appui,* you were never to forget that it was a problem. For the liberal intellectual everything, including life itself, is a problem which can be solved by the right mixture of good will, moderation and diligence. The situation was the same with the other forces which were shaping the kind of world we live in now. In 1946 I found myself unable to place anywhere an article arguing that a total surrender to technology would pollute the land and create such unnatural tensions that whole populations would be driven crazy because, as the editor of a famous American magazine (now defunct) wrote to my agent, "It is not our policy to encourage any ideas critical of science." And to rub the point well and truly into me, he added, "Your writer does not seem to realize that without science, democracy would not have been able to win the war."

I should have let it go at that. Though it is safer to argue with an editor than with a critic, any writer should have known better than to argue with an editor like this one. But I didn't know any better. I answered him that if Jellicoe had been the only man able to lose the First War in an afternoon, and had not done it, the geniuses who had made the A-bomb and the generals who had ordered it dropped had lost the entire meaning of their victory in the Second War in the instant of time it took the bomb to explode. I received no reply to this, nor did that magazine accept anything my agent sent to it afterwards.

And still another thing must be said about the character of these pieces. They were written during the only period of my entire life—seven long years, indeed—when I was totally out of touch with the young. Though their tone was mainly dictated by whatever the traffic would bear, my isolation from the young explains why such meager humour as these articles contain is as elephantine as a "funny" editorial in a metropolitan newspaper or an after-dinner speech re-read in tranquility.

By some quirk of a committee's judgment, *Cross-Country* was given a Governor General's Award in the days when the G.G. medal came to you without a cheque attached, for Canada's richest citizen had yet to die intestate and thereby endow the St. Laurent government with the funds to put culture into business through the Canada Council. You were presented with your medal after an hour or two of oratory succeeding the dinner that climaxed the annual convention of the Canadian Authors' Association, which was held in a different city every year. When *Cross-Country* was decorated I was too broke—I mean there wasn't that much cash in my bank account—to pay for the round trip to Winnipeg let alone my food and room when I got there, so a more solvent friend volunteered to accept the medal in my name and deliver it to me when he returned to Montreal. Let those who still despair of Canadian literature take heart from the knowledge that no book like this would win an award today.

Yet, in spite of all I have been saying, Mel Hurtig may

not be entirely mad in reviving this lost child. True, my re-reading of it comes after twenty years during which we lived with Joe McCarthy, Stalin, Synghman Rhee, the Dulles brothers, Duplessis, C. D. Howe, Eden, Nasser, Henry Luce, De Gaulle, the Mau Mau, Diefenbaker, the *Readers' Digest,* Castro, Bob Hope and Bing Crosby, Khrushchev, the CIA, Schmerz or whatever the Soviets call their equivalent of the CIA, Kim Philby, The FLQ, L. B. Johnson, Generals Twining, Lemay and Westmoreland, Brezhnev, the Beatles—but the list is already too long. Let me apologize to all whose names I have omitted and let the band play a *Te Deum* in celebration of the fact that the planet, planetarially speaking, is still intact. Anyway, though re-reading this little book gave me the lost feeling you get when you go to a college reunion, my mind does not entirely boggle at the idea that these pieces do have a certain value, humiliating though that value may be to a writer who has pride in his craftsmanship.

These are artifacts, genuine artifacts of Canadian and American attitudes in the last remaining years before the collective soul of puritan America exploded and blasted into outer space the devils and all the various outraged and love-deprived elements in its psyche which puritan will power had kept under lock and key for centuries. Even in their solemn, outdated style they are nostalgic of the time when you could always tell the difference between a boy and a girl when you walked through Yorkville, of the time before the young wasps swarmed and stung the parent wasps and it was not only possible, it was automatic, to believe that the United States was the last, best hope of mankind. "They told me, Heraclitus, they told me you were dead...." Or did my re-reading tell me something different, tell me perhaps, as I look around me now, hear around me now, sense around me now, that the children of Heracleitus have made up their souls to abandon his heritage in order to save life itself? Or does it tell me the opposite, that his society has already descended so deep into the bowels of its technology that it can't even crawl out backwards? I really don't know.

So an idea born, perhaps, out of nothing more respectable than an author's vanity repeats the hope that a few readers may find interest in these period pieces merely because of what an artifact can suggest to us about ourselves at the moment when we examine it. For here they are, once-acceptable, once-praised products of that transition into God knows what when the British Labour politicians were disencumbering themselves of their empire, when Mackenzie King still haunted Ottawa and blunted the national mind; when Winston Churchill was our universal father; when the veterans worked furiously to make up for lost time and give their children the blessings, chances and freedoms denied to themselves in the depression and the war; when the incredible Germans and Japanese—beaten, bombed and burned out, shamed even in their own eyes—in an uncanny silence set about rebuilding their ruined lands; when you could eat a first-class dinner at the Café Martin for $1.50 and in Toronto could drink nothing in public but beer; when in the same Montreal movie houses which now exhibit *I am Curious, Yellow* and *Initiation*, a married woman could not be kissed on the screen and the word "divorce" was taboo, when it was an uncomfortable adventure to fly the Atlantic and hardly anyone outside a rural district of Texas had heard of LBJ, when black was not yet beautiful and men's hair was cropped and women's dresses were long, when the entire city of Montreal turned on its lights to welcome its new and only Cardinal and the idea that Canada could ever produce a Leonard Cohen was, if not unthinkable, certainly unthought, even by Leonard himself. And one thing more. Though the word "radio" pops up all over this book, the word "television" is mentioned in one piece only.

The stuffiest article must surely be the first one. It was written on request for the American publication *Foreign Affairs*, prestigious in its field, and the idea was to offer in acceptable small-l liberal form polite answers to specific questions posed by the editor. When I read it over, wincing at line after line, I thought what a quantum-leap we have made in Canada since anyone could write a sentence like this and know it to be literally true: "In Quebec there is a much-used slogan, *notre maitre, le passé.*" Or this: "With the advent of Mr. St. Laurent . . . Canadian public life is a little less dilly than it was." Or this lame and impotent, but at the time of writing all too authentic an expression of representative liberal Canadianism both in style and content: "Though it cannot be too often repeated that Canadians like and respect the United States [can't you hear the voice of Lester Pearson?] few of them would consider that a world dominated by American methods and American materialism would be an unqualified blessing to mankind." The truth was, of course, that even while mouthing sentiments like these hundreds of thousands of Canadians were at that very moment on the springboard getting set to dive into the hog trough. But the worst is yet to come: "Canada is more than thankful that the leadership of Franklin Roosevelt led Americans out of their former immaturity in foreign affairs." Oh, my God, did I write that? "But her present orientation toward Washington does not imply a rejection of Great Britain. . . . " A little in this, maybe. "Even though Canadians recognize, as the British do themselves, that the centre of gravity has moved not only to Washington but to the whole North American continent. . . ."

After a sentence like this final one, please may I pause for what used to be called station identification? When I wrote those lines, incredible though it may seem, they were not totally platitudinous. Even as late as 1948 people were still conditioned to expect that all international crises, together with the power to create them, had their sources in Europe, and to apply the word "empire" to the United States was an unpardonable rudeness if not a confession of communism.

I suppose the best piece here, if you can use a superlative of any of them, is the short story called "An Orange From Portugal" which comes close to being founded on actual fact. The piece on Yosuf Karsh's *Faces Of Destiny* seemed fresh and even exciting at the time and despite the dubious argument of the first paragraph it might still be good were it not for this: since then television has so saturated us with the countenances of politicians and generals that any philosophical conclusions it contains have become as familiar as the Law of Gravity. And so on to the one the editors entitled "Elephant On Parade."

The convention held by the Republican Party in Philadelphia in 1948 was one of the most futile ever put together by that party, which takes in a lot of territory, yet paradoxically it was probably the most important political assembly held anywhere since Lenin gathered together his Bolsheviks under the roof of the Tauride Palace in Petrograd in 1917. The politicians behaved as I have described them and in some quarters I was severely criticized for lack of reverence to them; were they not, after all, defenders of democracy? Since then, of course, all of them with the possible exception of Henry Cabot Lodge have descended into a limbo so profound that their names have the nostalgic poignancy of names read on the tombstones of a small town cemetery. In that year the Republicans took it for granted that anyone they nominated, even Stassen who has been running for president ever since, was certain to occupy the White House, for the press and the polls had issued an almost unanimous guarantee that Truman was a goner. This fact—not Truman's being a goner but that the assembly of men spread out on the floor of that convention hall was plenipotentiary—seemed extremely alarming to me, especially after I had spent four days looking at them and hearing them talk. On the suffocating night when the names were at last put into nomination, I asked the journalist next to me in the periodicals section if he could give me his estimate of the background and calibre of the average delegate. He said it was a good question and he thought about it for nearly ten minutes before he gave his answer.

"Now I'm making no crack," he said, pointing down at more than two thousand delegates. "The common denominator down there has to come from the middle west, he's going to be physically big and somewhere around fifty years old. For his profession what would I go for? I'll take a chance and say horse doctor—but a good one."

Escaping from the Turkish bath of the hall into the air-conditioned cool of the press lounge, I recognized the tall, rangy figure of our own John George Diefenbaker and he looked like my idea of Slim in Steinbeck's *Of Mice and Men*. His hour of destiny was still nine years off in the future and the Honourable Member from Prince Albert was here as a spectator. We introduced ourselves and in return he introduced me to a man some three inches taller than himself with the eyelashes and expression of a highly bred bird dog, and as this man shook my hand he told me that anyone who was a friend of John was a friend of his.

"And now," he said, "tell me, do you know Doctor ———?" I forget the name he pronounced but remember that I had to admit that I had never heard of him.

The delegate—for that was what his badge said and he was from Indiana—then made a statement which seemed to me divinely inspired.

"I'm sorry you don't," he said. "We folks down here in the veterinary profession of the United States recognize that your Doctor ——— is just about as wonderful as you can find anywhere."

In the article I described this delegate from Indiana as a nice man. He was. And my recollections of our short conversation make me wish there had been at least six hundred delegates half as good at the conventions in Miami and Chicago in 1968.

But the real importance of this otherwise barren convention eluded us all. It so happened that this was the first occasion in the world when the TV cameras were turned onto a political assembly and though it was estimated that no more than 60,000 people saw the show— sets were just coming into production and there were not even coaxial cables—it was on that night that television won its spurs, if that is the correct word to apply to a medium which may yet turn out more dangerous than the bubonic plague. As I sat in the lounge watching the little screen it never even crossed my mind that I was witnessing a phenomenon that was going to shake the foundations of all traditional government. For as the word went round that the convention could be seen on television, more politicians entered the lounge to stare at the box and then it was that they discovered that on that little screen they were more real and impressive than they could ever be in their all-too-palpable flesh. So, as Malcolm Muggeridge was to observe many years later, our collective lives were turned inside out. Instead of the world being the stage, the stage became the world. How odd that Marshall McLuhan, whose insight discovered this instantly, should have believed it a blessing!

As for my last two efforts, the one on religion and the one called "The Tyranny of the Sunday Suit," more people read the religious one than anything else I ever wrote for a Canadian magazine. Once again a re-reading throws what now is a very obvious article into a wry perspective. Except in Quebec, South Africa and the Bible Belt, it was generally admitted in 1948 that religion was a waning force and most intellectuals agreed that the sooner it disappeared the better. Yet at the same time the majority of people regretted its going and the PRs of the Eisenhower government a few years later believed they could get a good deal of mileage out of its revival, which they sought to do by identifying Christianity with anti-communism and American patriotism. For a while during the trance of the fifties the idea seemed to be working pretty well for them. Television cameras were dutifully set up close to the portals of the Presbyterian Church to catch Eisenhower going in to worship and Norman Vincent Peale was not the only one of the various journalistic clergymen who exploited the trend and grew rich on it. Even as late as 1960, Richard Nixon was able to declare in his acceptance speech, without being sued either by his parents or by any religious denomination in America, that "All I am I owe to my parents, my family and my church." This may explain why he came within a few hundred thousand votes of winning the prize from John F. Kennedy in 1960. When he finally made it eight years later he was careful to leave the churches out of his campaign, at least on national television for if any politician allies himself with Christianity these days he is likely to be considered an enemy of sex and the young if not actually a racist. It is very curious. Now, with the churches all but empty shells, the hunger for a believable religion may well be stronger than at any time in world history since the reign of Caracalla. How otherwise explain Woodstock? And as we are so much the creatures of our own desires, as it is imagination rather than speech which differentiates us from all other living creatures, it seems certain to me that after a time God is sure to displace the sphinx, though in what form He comes nobody seems able to guess and few would even try.

As for the last article in this book, it is the kind of journalism whose message is as dead as a fossil and for this nobody is more thankful than myself. There are still a handful of politicians in our midst, some of them prominent, who speak to us as though they had just come out of church and that is why, for all their rectitude and intelligence, they lose elections. Well, as H. G. Wells sadly remarked in his old age as he surveyed a shelf of his own books, the trouble with good journalism is that if it is successful it kills itself.

Regardless of what the critics have said, I have never sought to convert anyone to anything in my novels. I think they are honest all-out products of my authentic neuroses and compulsions, even of my excitements and joy in life and nature and if the early ones contained more explanatory material than is acceptable today, the reason was not a desire to proselytize, but the necessity of defining and making at least partly visible a Canadian psychological landscape which in those days was virtually unexplored. But in these particular essays and in others I have written since, I did write deliberate journalism because I loved this country and found it fascinating and sickened to see its spokesmen constantly and wrongly describing it in the terms of foreigners and seeking to see it through strangers' eyes. It disgusted me to witness year after year the subservience of news writers who refused to accept a good Canadian writer or actor before he had made his name and a lot of money in New York or Hollywood, or to listen on radio to those dreary panels where representative Canadians argued whether or not Canada was dull, or whether it was worth paying the price of being Canadian—as late as the early 1960s "The Price Of Being Canadian" was the title of a Couchiching Winter Conference. I think worst of all was the intellectual snobbery you encountered in universities where literature professors seemed to feel that if they admitted that a Canadian writer or artist, writing or painting out of the Canadian experience, was capable of work of real value, they would label themselves as provincials and from this attitude was born the present so-called controversy among the critics between what they call "national" writing and "cosmopolitan" writing. The distinction seemed to me then, as it does now, entirely artificial and unreal. A novelist writes of what he knows best and often of what he loves best and this means that with hardly any exceptions, the most cosmopolitan writers in history have written out of their own countries. Now from my association over recent years with thousands of young people, I am convinced that for the majority of them the evolution has finally occurred and that if books and poetry written by Canadians are acceptable, it is not because they are Canadian but because they are good and interesting books.

I think therefore that it is this evolution which has changed the value of these pieces in *Cross-Country* into the kind of value we discover in fossils and that is the whole point I have been trying to make. I am grateful to Mel Hurtig for giving me the chance to be my own reviewer for a change and I hope I have been an honest one. I am at least honest enough to admit that I would never have exposed a book like this to modern reviewers without having had my own crack at it first.

HUGH MACLENNAN

North Hatley, Quebec
July 1970

PREFACE

THERE is no obvious cohesion between the various essays in this collection, nor has any subtle unity been hidden in the pages. Yet they have a strong inter-relationship, not only because they were written by one man within the few years since the end of the Second World War, but also because in each instance the writing of them taught me something it was necessary to know before I could advance with my principal work, the writing of novels.

The fact that all of us have been reaching for new definitions during this period of time, seeking to understand new alignments which have been forced upon us by necessity, may indicate that one man's waymarks are not so different from those of his neighbour. However, the definitions I have formulated in these essays are my own and I make no attempt to say that I am a Canadian speaking for Canadians. I speak for myself alone.

Were I to do these pieces over again today I should like
to think I could handle some of them in a lighter vein,
but I am probably wrong, inasmuch as they are the
searchings of a man who has developed slowly into some
understanding of the transitional nature of the period in
which he happens to live. Even on second thoughts,
that period is not especially funny.

As a substitute for trying to write them over again, I
have given each essay a short introduction, not to take
advantage of hindsight but to add perspective. Sooner
or later most writers make the discovery that no book or
article to which they have signed their names has any
existence in reality until it has been in the hands of the
public for a certain length of time. When that happens
it ceases to belong to the author, and he finds he can talk
about his work as though it had been written by someone
else. At times he can even free himself of a strong
prejudice in its favour. I am in that happy position at
the moment.

Some of the titles of these essays have been retained as
they appeared originally in print; others I have changed
because the names by which they made their initial
appearance were not of my choosing or even liking. The
reading public, I have discovered, never ceases to show
surprise upon learning that titles of books as well as of
magazine articles usually reflect the tastes of editors.
I make no complaint; I am as often pleased as annoyed
by an editor's choice. But the purposes of this book are
not the purposes of a popular magazine.

I should also like to place on record a continuing debt
to my wife, Dorothy Duncan, who edited each of these
articles before their original submission for publication.
I hesitate to think how some of them would have read
without her help, for a man with a philosophic twist to

his mind seldom finds it easy to say clearly what he is thinking. I start out well enough, but every idea set down produces its own tangents in my mind and I can never resist the temptation to explore each by-path as it appears. Before I know it, I am miles off the point, with no sense of having traversed anything but a logical straight line on the way to a conclusion.

Dorothy is invariably capable of tripping me with a well-timed series of hows and whys, and what is more, she stays with me until I have produced a piece which she feels is the best I can do at the time. More than that a writer can ask of no editor on earth.

Permission to reprint these essays has been granted by the publications named on p. xxv. In parentheses I have indicated the names of corresponding chapters in this book in every case where a title has been changed.

The Psychology of Canadian Nationalism: *Foreign Affairs;* New York, April, 1949. (The Canadian Character)

An Orange from Portugal: *Chatelaine;* Toronto, December, 1948.

How We Differ from Americans: *Maclean's;* Toronto, December 15, 1946. (On Discovering Who We Are)

The Face of Power: *Maclean's;* Toronto, May 1, 1947.

What Does Uncle Sam Want?: *Maclean's;* Toronto, April 1, 1948. (Cross-Country)

Halifax: *National Home Monthly;* Toronto, April, 1949. (Portrait of a City)

The Elephant on Parade: *Maclean's;* Toronto, August 15, 1948.

Are We a Godless People?: *Maclean's;* Toronto, March 15, 1949. ("Help Thou Mine Unbelief")

The Tyranny of the Sunday Suit: An address to the Canadian Club of Toronto, November, 1948.

CONTENTS

High-spirited friend,
I send nor balms nor cor'sives to your wound:
Your fate hath found
A gentler and more agile hand to tend
The cure of that which is but corporal;
And doubtful days, which were named critical,
Have made their fairest flight
And now are out of sight.
Yet doth some wholesome physic for the mind
Wrapped in this paper lie,
Which in the taking if you misapply
You are unkind.

—BEN JONSON

CROSS-
COUNTRY

I

THE
CANADIAN CHARACTER

The subject of this article is a peg on which I have been trying to hang my hat for years. Other essays in this book—notably On Discovering Who We Are—*indicate earlier attempts to reach a conclusion on the same subject, but it was not until I had finished this particular essay for* Foreign Affairs *that I felt I had said all I wanted to say for the time being about the wellsprings of the Canadian national character.*

Those who believe there is no such thing as the psychology of a nation will find nothing but items with which to disagree in this article, for it is my argument that a national character does exist in Canada, even as I maintain that it is notably different from the character of most individual Canadians.

Inasmuch as this piece was written specifically for an American publication at the request of its editor, Mr. Hamilton Armstrong, it contains several explanations which could have been taken for granted had I been writing for Canadians alone. But it will probably do no harm to review them if we remember that the national behaviour of the Dominion is being scrutinized more closely than ever before, respectfully, I am assured, but still with scant understanding. How could it be otherwise when we have done so little to make ourselves known to the rest of the world?

THE CANADIAN CHARACTER

IN THE autumn of 1948 William Lyon Mackenzie King completed his inch-by-inch retirement from public life as Prime Minister of Canada. He had finally served as head of state for a longer time than had any president, prime minister, consul or archon in the history of democracy, and on the way he had broken several longstanding records of other ministers of the British Crown.

These records apparently meant a lot to Mr. King. Each one that was broken was followed by rumours of his retirement, but the rumours were never specifically denied and Mr. King continued in office, his memory counting the tenure of his service to the hour. Then retirement was forced upon him suddenly one day for the reason of failing health. It was unfortunate that his own studied technique of doing everything as unobtrusively as possible had trained people to expect from him nothing dramatic, nothing that stimulates the imagination, nothing that suggests a crisis. Had he been an American, had he been an Englishman, had he been anything but the kind of Canadian he is, the record he set would have been celebrated with pomp at home and careful examination in other countries. As it was, the announcement of his retirement was noted by the world's press with only such interest as politeness required.

Mr. King's career, no less than the irony implicit in the quietness of his retirement from it, is deeply symbolic of the country he governed. Under his leadership, Canada has developed into the fourth military power among the United Nations, and subsequently into the second most important economic reservoir of western democracy. Few nations in modern times have grown in stature more rapidly. Canada has long ceased to be a Dominion in the original sense of the word; nor has she now, in swinging away from Great Britain, become what so many feared was inevitable, an appendage of the United States. She has become a highly integrated, growing nation, lacking one attribute only which seems necessary for world recognition. Like Mr. King himself, Canada has such a talent for avoiding the dramatic that she too often escapes even the notice of her friends.

What do most outsiders think of when the image of a Canadian comes to mind? Usually of a trooper of the Royal Canadian Mounted Police in dress of scarlet, solitary on horseback surveying the Rocky Mountains. Sometimes of a trapper, of a hard-rock miner, of a kilted soldier playing the bagpipes at a Toronto fair, of a rawboned sportsman who is the salt of the earth but notably unsubtle. On certain levels they remember the competent, mild-mannered, well-dressed individuals, neither British nor American but oddly reminiscent of both nationalities, who represent Canada at international con-

4

ferences. In any event, Canadians are thought of as preëminently masculine, and this is fair enough; in both public and family life it is the men who are dominant in Canada. A masculine common sense, even a masculine lack of sensitivity, reveals itself in every facet of Canadian life from architecture to food. But the very truth of this fact has diverted nearly everyone who has tried to make visible the psychology of Canada as a nation.

As has often been pointed out, a nation is an abstraction. It is a convenient word or image which we use when we mean a group psychology, a group behaviour-pattern or a group policy. And here is the paradox which has caused Canada to be so often misunderstood. Canada, *as a nation*, is not masculine at all. She is feminine. This feminine psychology has not arisen out of the lives of individual Canadians nor out of the kind of country they inhabit. It came into being because a country with Canada's peculiar history happens to share the major part of the North American continent with a colossus like the United States. Were it not for the United States, Canada would never have been a nation at all, much less the kind she is.

This country, which once was Britain's senior Dominion and now stands on her own, has acquired a purely feminine capacity for sustaining within her nature contradictions so difficult to reconcile that most societies possessing them would be torn by periodic revolutions. Canada has acquired a good woman's hatred of quarrels, the good woman's readiness to make endless compromises for the sake of peace within the home, the good woman's knowledge that although her husband can knock her down if he chooses, she will be able to make him ashamed of himself if such an idea begins to form in his mind. Canada also possesses the hard rock which is in the core of every good woman's soul: any threat to her basic values calls up a reluctant but implacable resistance.

This national feminine psychology becomes amusingly obvious in the attitude of the country towards the United States. Canadians have always clucked their tongues at American flamboyance and recklessness, but they know that life would be drab without them. They watch with indulgent amusement, even while affecting disapproval, the delight Americans take in their own accomplishments, their freedom from inhibitions, their love of boasting, their penchant for getting into the kind of trouble a lesser people would avoid and their correspondingly noisy vigour in getting out of it. During the past fifty or sixty years, Canadians have enjoyed the United States much as a good wife enjoys the spectacle of a robust husband being himself.

Another aspect of Canada's feminine psychology is seen in the manner in which her whole career as a nation has been a sort of domestic defiance of the United States. Her history shows that her dominant national impulse is to retain in her own eyes the kind of personality she *feels* she has, even though she has never been able to define this personality in words. Although she is pleased when Americans recognize her good qualities, she has never sued for American favour because she has been too proud to make the slightest effort to express herself in terms which might lead Americans to believe that she values their good opinion too highly.

The economist and the sociologist find different methods of explaining the psychology of Canada, but with a few notable exceptions, they generally require from the foreign reader more skill in coördinating abstractions than any human being is likely to possess.

Economists tell us that there is no real basis of economic

6

union in Canada. The wheat-producing provinces have generally felt themselves treated like a colonial empire by the large eastern cities. The Maritime Provinces, with their tradition of seafaring and free trade, bitterly resent the tariffs imposed on them by the more populous manufacturing areas of Ontario and Quebec. In addition, many of Canada's most vital industries are controlled in the United States. Sociologists have constantly emphasized that Canadians have no common tradition of patriotism or even of social values. The English-speaking majority and the French-speaking minority are divided not only by religion and language, but are descended from ancestors who once were bitter national enemies, and whose struggles are remembered with deep emotion.

Those Canadians who are their own sharpest critics have attempted to explain the national character in terms of a sizeable inferiority complex. They talk about the reticence of their fellow-countrymen—both individually and as a national group—their reluctance to tell the rest of the world what a fine country Canada is. They deplore the behaviour-pattern of a proud people who still react to the well-grounded belief that no matter how much they may contribute to a common cause, neither Britain nor the United States will accord them proper recognition. But these are only shadows on the picture. There are still more sides to this complex Canadian personality. The people of the country have also been strongly affected by physical environment, by a mixed religious inheritance, and by the invasion of American ideas from Hollywood and New York. These, too, have made her what she is.

The climate of Canada allows for less margin of error in economic life than does the climate of the United States. The average Canadian farmer is poorer than the average

7

American farmer by at least five weeks of warm weather. Moreover, there is only a narrow belt of land—all of it lying close to the American border—which is uniformly fertile. The rest of the Dominion is mostly bush, tundra, hard-rock shield and ice cap. To be sure, Canada appears to be a nation of still untapped wealth so far as mineral resources are concerned, but since man has not yet learned to eat gold and pitchblende, wealth in such terms must be reckoned in basic values.

In addition to the repressions enforced by nature, there are few nations in which established religion has had a greater success in curbing exuberances. The authority of the Quebec priest over his parish is famous. In the English-speaking provinces Calvinism has been endemic from the beginning. Although both religions have done much to fortify Canadian society in the face of geographical debits, they have enormously inhibited the Canadian character in the process.

Finally, Canadian psychology within the last few generations has been subtly but thoroughly worked on by American motion pictures, American radio programmes, American books, advertising in American magazines—a series of pressures which we Canadians have not so far returned in kind. For want of a true native culture which is dramatic enough to compete with New York and Hollywood, we have allowed ourselves to absorb that of the United States. As a result, we have tended to understand Americans *intellectually* better than we understand ourselves.

The more one enters into such detail, the more confused the picture becomes. Canada has two official languages, yet the resources of both have failed to provide a single word to designate a citizen of the country. When those of the French language use the word *Canadien*, they refer

8

only to themselves; the rest of the population are *les Anglais*. Those who speak English operate on the same principle. *They* are the "Canadians;" the qualifying word "French-Canadian" is reserved for the inhabitants of Quebec. To date, Canada has no official flag. One of the hottest debates in recent parliamentary history occurred when the project of adopting a national flag was raised and discarded after weeks of exasperated argument. George VI is king of Canada; yet Canada is not a dependency of Great Britain. Canadians have no wish to join the United States, but they are almost more concerned by American national elections than by their own.

In spite of such contradictions, Canada is probably the most stable country in the world. Her standard of living is second only to that of the United States, and a close second at that. Canadians are more law-abiding than Americans, they are conservative no matter to which language group they belong; yet—as their social legislation proves—they are not reactionary. When Mr. King retired and handed the leadership to Mr. Louis St. Laurent, there was no perceptible change in internal or international policy. Mr. St. Laurent, a Roman Catholic of Quebec, continued calmly where Mr. King, an Ontario Presbyterian, had left off. One can only conclude, therefore, that Canada must contain some invisible common denominator which has kept her people stable and has drawn them together politically in spite of the dichotomies of which she is composed.

Canada became a nation through the coöperation of two distinctly different kinds of people, reinforced by a third group which had nothing in common with the social background of the other two. The first two were the French, who were the original European inhabitants of the country, and the United Empire Loyalists, of English stock from the Thirteen Colonies. The third group were Highland Scots. In subsequent years there were immigrations from Ulster, southern Ireland, England, Scotland, Wales and the continent of Europe, but it is extraordinary how little these later settlers altered the psychological mould which was set in Canada in the early days. They never counteracted the vital fact that the three original settling groups became Canadians because the nations or factions to which they had belonged had suffered total defeat in war. It was in their response to the challenge of these three separate defeats, a response which in each case was remarkably similar, that the common denominator in the Canadian character was forged.

In French-Canada today there is a much-used slogan, *notre maître, le passé*. The glorious past of French-Canada has overshadowed her immediate present ever since 1763. The greatest names in Canadian history—indeed, in the early history of the North American continent—are all French. What men can historians of the English colonies set up against Cartier, Champlain, Cavelier de la Salle, Père Marquette, Brébeuf, Joliet, d'Iberville, Radisson, Frontenac, Laval and Montcalm? Such names ring like bugle calls across the whole of America. Always working with fewer resources, both of men and materials, handicapped by corrupt governments in France, unsupported by sea power, the French under such leaders more than held their own against superior odds for a century and a half. And then suddenly their glory and their hope collapsed.

After the fall of Quebec in the Seven Years' War, the inhabitants of New France found themselves without a mother country. By the Treaty of Paris in 1763, France formally abandoned them to England, their hereditary

10

foe.   Sixty-five thousand Frenchmen of Catholic Norman stock, most of whom had been born in Lower Canada, found themselves alone in a hostile, Protestant, English-speaking continent, helpless before their conquerors' whims.   Voltaire, in a cheap epigram, wrote of the country for which they had fought and suffered as "a few acres of ice and snow."   Not only were the French-Canadians robbed of a mother country when France deserted them, they were robbed of one of the greatest dreams ever cherished by a human society, the dream of a French-speaking Roman Catholic empire extending from Gaspé to the Gulf of Mexico.

After receiving such a blow from the British, why did the French-Canadians, barely sixteen years after the fall of Quebec, choose to remain under the British flag when the seceding American colonies sent Benjamin Franklin to beg them to join their revolution?

To answer this riddle is to explain how French-Canada met the challenge of her defeat.   Two years before the outbreak of the American Revolution, the British Government had passed the famous Quebec Act, the most liberal political document enacted by a conqueror up to that time.   It guaranteed the French-Canadians freedom of religion, the right to preserve their own language in the courts and to teach it in the schools, as well as the right to continue the use and practice of French civil law.   In addition to the official attitude of the British Government, as expressed in the Act, the first British governors happened to have been humane, chivalrous and intelligent men.

In contrast to the behaviour of the British, the attitude of such Americans as the French had known was deplorable.   In the colonial wars it had been Americans who had insisted on the expulsion of the Acadians, and Americans who had treated Louisburg like a modern Carthage. Immediately after the fall of Quebec, New Englanders had swarmed north in the hope of despoiling the new province. They were bitter Protestants, intolerant of any aims or values but their own. Now, in 1776, the Catholic hierarchy let it be known that they regarded with abhorrence the principles behind the revolution.

In this great crisis in continental history, the attitude of French-Canadians hardened into a mould which has remained distinct to this day. After the Quebec Act was passed, the only aims they had left were to survive ethnically, to remain defenders of the Catholic faith and the French legend in North America, to preserve in so far as they could the tradition of their mighty ancestors. Then and now, they accepted the realities of their position. Their Norman common sense has continually enabled them to recognize what was to become a real principle in Canadian political life: when choices are few, take half a loaf and remember it is better than no bread.

It was a supreme irony of history which soon thereafter caused the French-Canadians to share Canada with tens of thousands of the very Yankee Protestants they had hitherto detested more than any other people on earth, the Loyalists in the colonies who had sided with the mother country during the Revolution. These people— men, women and children—were hounded north into the wilderness of Ontario and the Maritime Provinces, bounding Quebec on both sides, by the self-righteous rage of their own blood-relations.

Professor Toynbee has pointed out that no people in the history of Christendom had up to this time suffered such a fate for purely *political* opinions. The Loyalists were still Yankee in character and Protestant in religion. Their decision to remain loyal to England might have been wrong, but it had been as sincerely formed as was the decision of the others to revolt. Their treatment at the hands of their former countrymen, followed as it was by the virtual indifference of the British to their plight once the war was lost, produced in their collective psychology a kind of traumatic shock. They never gave way to the self-pity which was to retard the recovery of the American South a century later, nor did they glorify the legend of their own past. They had too much to do and too much to learn to brood upon it, since most of them came from a settled environment and now found themselves pioneers in a cold, unbroken country. As their social culture developed through the years it was seen to be more rigid than that of the United States, more cautious, less optimistic, more close-mouthed. In the early days, few of them expected Canada to amount to much and they retained their old dislike of Quebec. But they were determined to survive as British subjects in North America; like the French, they had made up their minds that half a loaf is better than no bread at all.

The third racial group, the Highlanders, became Canadians as a result of the infatuated loyalty of their chiefs to Charles Edward Stuart. After Culloden, while Charles did his best to drink himself into forgetfulness of his helpless dupes, the British set out ruthlessly to break down the clan system. This policy was later followed by enclosures, and when it became increasingly difficult for the clansmen to get a living in the Highlands, whole villages departed in communal ships for Canada. They settled in small, closely-knit communities in the Maritimes, in Ontario and even in Quebec, and, though they retained the Gaelic, they quickly set out to learn English. Few peoples, with the possible exception of the Japanese, have ever accommodated themselves more rapidly to the methods of European civilization. They remembered their past, but in a spirit which Santayana would commend, for they had no intention of repeating it. Loyal by tradition and nature they might be, but they would never again be loyal in the suicidal spirit of Cameron of Lochiel.

Thus, if the members of each of these original groups which settled Canada had been able to voice their feelings in the hour of their tragedy, they would have spoken identical words: "Never again will we submit ourselves to the humiliation of being discarded by the friends for whom we were prepared to give everything we had."

For a time the distinct sections of what came to be known as British North America were governed as individual colonies of Great Britain. And then the growing pains of the American Republic caused a series of crises which directly affected these provinces to the north. Through their response to these new challenges they finally became a self-governing Dominion with a national psychology based directly on the past history of the three original groups.

The first crisis was the War of 1812. American armies were repulsed from their invasion of Canadian soil by the joint efforts of the Loyalists and the French-Canadians, assisted by small bodies of British regulars. For Canada, it was a decisive victory.

The second crisis was precipitated by President Polk over the question of the western boundary. Canadians were once more prepared to fight if invaded. War was averted, but Polk's imperialism made the Loyalists and the French realize that they had more to gain by standing together than by bickering.

The third and most serious crisis arose out of the resentment felt by Americans against the British at the time of the Civil War. Even before Lincoln's first inauguration, Canadians had viewed Seward with justifiable alarm. Their apprehensions reached a climax when the war ended and Lincoln's restraining influence was removed. Some American statesmen talked openly of annexing Canada in reprisal for British "violations" of neutrality during the Civil War. The American action of terminating the Reciprocity Treaty of 1854 was viewed by British North America as a direct threat. The answer of the provinces was to form, in 1867, the Confederation which made Canada a nation in fact, with a federal parliament of her own. Thus, without meaning to do so, the United States brought about the establishment of a nation composed of peoples who had no desire to unite, but who— true to the lesson their respective pasts had taught them— chose union with each other in preference to absorption by another state which would care nothing for the respective heritages they cherished.

It was in the years following Confederation that the present era of friendship and good will between Canada and the United States began. Confederation proved to American statesmen that Canada was not a military outpost of Great Britain, and with the departure of suspicion on one side and fear on the other, the sentiments of Canadians rapidly warmed to their southern neighbour. The puritan descendants of the Loyalists, now that the slaves were liberated, were at last willing to admit that the Revolution had been not only successful, but had been fought with loftier motives than to keep Sam Adams and John Hancock out of jail. Although Great Britain was respected and even loved by English-Canada, and though loyalty to the Crown was inculcated in the schools, Canadians were always conscious of being North Americans.

Now the great saga of continental development was

being celebrated by American writers and propagandists, soon to be followed by American motion pictures and radio, and this saga was part of the blood and bone of the Canadian people. American spokesmen constantly expressed ideas and emotions which Canadians shared. The analogy to the good wife appears once more. A man triumphs over great adversities, he civilizes a wilderness, he becomes rich and performs feats that stupefy the world. He boasts and glories in his achievement, and the world recognizes and honours him. His wife remains silent, but she knows in her heart that to more than a small extent his story is also her own.

So much for the good wife analogy. One returns inevitably to the career of William Lyon Mackenzie King, because he must be explained, at least in part, in any study of Canada today. This solitary bachelor with the tufted eyebrows, with a voice like that of a Presbyterian minister and a face which contrives to be both well-plumped and rugged at the same time, has done more than retain personal power for a record number of years. He is one of the few constructive political geniuses of the century. The fact that his face, as he has grown older, has assumed the expression of a watchdog pretending to be meek and melancholy is no accident.

During a good part of the Second World War, Mr. King was probably the most unpopular man in Canada. It was his aim to keep Canada united, to enable her to work for victory in the widest sense of the term, and to guide her towards a larger, independent development as a nation. For six years he walked the tight-rope with confidence because he knew that the maintenance of social stability is, in Canada, a categorical imperative. He knew that no matter how deep lie the emotions of the people, no matter how profound their frustrations,

16

French and English alike have an overriding common aim upon which the Canadian national character, whatever its individual manifestations may be, firmly rests. Both groups know subconsciously that the security their ancestors lost so dramatically, and which their descendants so painfully regained, must be preserved at any price. Again and again, Canadians have shown that whenever their emotions come into conflict with this principle, the principle will prevail.

In the autumn of 1944, during what came to be known as the Conscription Crisis, the emotions of English-Canada were represented by the late Colonel Ralston, Minister of Defence. All thought they knew the French point of view: Quebec threatened secession if conscription were imposed. Mr. King, remembering how badly national unity had been bruised by the conscription bill of 1917, contrived by various dexterities to postpone the issue as long as enlistments were meeting needs. But in 1944 it could be postponed no longer. Mounting casualties had struck the nation with grief and threatened the effectiveness of the army.

The real issue at stake—whether or not the nation should permit the generous volunteer to assume an extra burden of danger which compulsory service might mitigate—was kept by the Prime Minister as far in the background as possible. His technical skill in doing this reached the levels of necromancy, for at this period the puritan conscience of English-Canada was working overtime. Colonel Ralston was embittered because he felt that a moral wrong was being committed before his eyes. The issue *should* stand forth. The nation should face its own conscience at home if it was afterwards to face its returned volunteers.

In the eyes of English-Canada, Ralston became a hero

overnight. His rôle was infinitely more popular than the Prime Minister's could possibly be, and he was totally sincere. Mr. King's behaviour at this time was respected by hardly anyone; yet, when passions subsided, it was recognized that he had displayed a moral courage of the most difficult kind, for it was the essence of his position that he had to make himself appear to the public to be less of a man than his antagonist, vacillating and weak while inwardly he not only knew himself to be right, but to be the strongest man in the country. Colonel Ralston so forcefully opposed Mr. King's policy of temporizing that his resignation was demanded by the Prime Minister. General MacNaughton, whose devotion to the army was unquestioned, for a few days seemed to be in agreement with Mr. King. The issue became too clouded for emotional intensity to find any direct outlet. Thus Mr. King, by playing on the national psychology with the skill of a magician, managed to save everything at once: the unbroken continuance of the war effort, the life of the government, national unity and his own place in history. The bill was passed in such a way that the English got their reinforcements, while the French, though losing on the actual issue, were able to feel that their stand on conscription had not only been morally right, but that English-Canada was grateful to them for having sacrificed their principles for the sake of national unity. Even Colonel Ralston, still a member of Parliament though out of the Cabinet, suppressed the enormous emotion he was feeling during the tense debate on the issue and conducted himself with calm dignity. He uttered no word against Quebec, he cast no slur on the integrity of the Prime Minister's tactics even when he most abhorred them. He was sufficiently Canadian to know that he himself, like his fellow-countrymen of both races, could never take the ultimate action which would wreck Confederation.

Mr. King's entire career has been marked by such feats, and there is no doubt that Canada owes much of her present stature to his strange species of resolution. Unfortunately, there is a debit side to his influence. In all of his public utterances he has described Canada in terms so uninteresting that only a man with superhuman determination could have kept the pattern so consistent. He never allowed anyone else to speak for him in the press, he discouraged photographers, he reduced to the barest minimum all attempts to dramatize Canada's rôle in the war. He must clearly have felt that the growing exuberance of a people awakening at last to their own strength and to a new vision of their country's beauties was dangerous.

Habits of thought are as difficult to break in nations as in individuals. Although Mr. King has encouraged some of the ablest young men in the country to enter public life, the effect of his ponderous insistence on removing all human contrasts and colour from political activity will be reflected in Canada's relations with other countries for some time to come. But it will not last forever. Strong forces from outside are helping strong forces from within. Canadians of the younger generation are much less inhibited than their parents. With the advent of Mr. St. Laurent—an urbane, integrated man of great personal charm—Canadian public life already seems less chilly than it was. A considerable body of art and literature is beginning to be recognized as the visible, articulate expression of a new facet of the national character. Canadians are thus feeding their own hungry longing for self-expression and self-realization, and a wider understanding on the part of the rest of the world is bound to follow.

The same basic principle which has guided Canada through the maelstrom of local emotions into nationhood is today the basis of her foreign policy. Though it cannot be repeated too often that Canadians like and respect the United States, few of them would consider that a world dominated wholly by American methods and American materialism would be an unqualified blessing for mankind. Canada is more than thankful that the leadership of Franklin Roosevelt led Americans out of their former immaturity in international affairs, but her present orientation towards Washington does not imply a rejection of Great Britain. Canadians recognize, as the British do themselves, that the centre of gravity has moved not only to Washington, but to the whole North American continent.

The day when the Canadian character could be adequately represented by mounted policemen, husky dogs, trappers, scenery and big game has disappeared. Canadians may seem to the world to be less colourful figures than their own tourist advertisements make them out to be, but American statesmen who frequent international conferences have been known to say that they feel more at ease with Canadians than with the representatives of any other nation. Of course they do. Instinctively, if not consciously, they know that Canadians understand their motives completely; their neighbours to the north are probably the only people in the world who regard the United States with a respect untainted by so much as a single grain of envy.

20

2

AN ORANGE FROM PORTUGAL

There are no afterthoughts in which to wrap this story, except a statement of my own pleasure in writing it.   Nothing in real life happens quite as neatly as the events I have related at the end, yet the piece as a whole is too factual to be termed a work of fiction. Individuals who take part in this story have no memory for the incidents I relate.   Nor do they feel that the rooms in which we were forced to live temporarily after our house blew up give an adequate representation of the background of my early life. Perhaps not, but the memory of those rooms remains vivid to me for the very reason that they were unusual and separate from the continuing pattern of the rest of my life in Halifax.   A novelist should never be asked to talk about his childhood if what is desired is a scientifically accurate report.   Nothing happens in his later years to compare with the impressions and emotions which flooded him when everything he saw was as new as if nobody had ever seen it before.

AN ORANGE FROM PORTUGAL

I suppose all of us, when we think of Christmas, recall Charles Dickens and our own childhood. So today, from an apartment in Montreal, looking across the street to a new neon sign, I think back to Dickens and Halifax and the world suddenly becomes smaller, shabbier and more comfortable, and one more proof is registered that comfort is a state of mind, having little to do with the number of springs hidden inside your mattress or the upholstery in your car.

Charles Dickens should have lived in Halifax. If he had, that brown old town would have acquired a better reputation in Canada than it now enjoys, for all over the world people would have known what it was like. Halifax, especially a generation or two ago, was a town Dickens could have used.

There were dingy basement kitchens all over the town where rats were caught every day. The streets were full of teamsters, hard-looking men with lean jaws, most of them, and at the entrance to the old North Street Station cab drivers in long coats would mass behind a heavy anchor chain and terrify travellers with bloodcurdling howls as they bid for fares. Whenever there was a southeast wind, harbour bells moaned behind the wall of fog that cut the town off from the rest of the world. Queer faces peered at you suddenly from doorways set flush with the streets. When a regiment held a smoker in the old Masonic Hall you could see a line beginning to form in the early morning, waiting for the big moment at midnight when the doors would be thrown open to the town and any man could get a free drink who could reach the hogsheads.

For all these things Dickens would have loved Halifax, even for the pompous importers who stalked to church on Sunday mornings, swinging their canes and complaining that they never had a chance to hear a decent sermon. He would have loved it for the waifs and strays and beachcombers and discharged soldiers and sailors whom the respectable never seemed to notice, for all the numerous aspects of the town that made Halifax deplorable and marvellous.

If Dickens had been given a choice of a Canadian town in which to spend Christmas, that's where I think he would have gone, for his most obvious attitude toward Christmas was that it was necessary. Dickens was no scientist or organizer. Instead of liking The People, he simply liked people. And so, inevitably, he liked places where accidents were apt to happen. In Halifax accidents were happening all the time. Think of the way he writes about Christmas—a perfect Christmas for him was always a chapter of preposterous accidents. No, I don't think he would have chosen to spend his Christmas in Westmount or Toronto, for he'd be fairly sure that neither of those places needed it.

Today we know too much. Having become democratic by ideology, we are divided into groups which eye each other like dull strangers at a dull party, polite in public and nasty when each others' backs are turned. Today we are informed by those who know that if we tell children about Santa Claus we will probably turn them into neurotics. Today we believe in universal justice and in universal war to effect it, and because Santa Claus gives the rich more than he gives the poor, lots of us think it better that there should be no Santa Claus at all. Today we are technicians, and the more progressive among us see no reason why love and hope should not be organized in a department of the government, planned by a politician and administered by trained specialists. Today we have a super-colossal Santa Claus for The Customer: he sits in the window of a department store in a cheap red suit, stringy whiskers and a mask which is a caricature of a face, and for a month before every Christmas he laughs continually with a vulgar roar. The sounds of his laughter come from a record played over and over, and the machine in his belly that produces the bodily contortions has a number in the patent office in Washington.

In the old days in Halifax we never thought about the meaning of the word democracy; we were all mixed up together in a general deplorability. So the only service any picture of those days can render is to help prove how far we have advanced since then. The first story I have to tell has no importance and not even much of a point. It is simply the record of how one boy felt during a Christmas that now seems remote enough to belong to the era of Tom Cratchit. The second story is about the same. The war Christmases I remember in Halifax were not jolly ones. In a way they were half-tragic, but there may be some significance in the fact that they are literally the only ones I can still remember. It was a war nobody down there understood. We were simply a part of it, swept into it from the mid-Victorian age in which we were all living until 1914.

On Christmas Eve in 1915 a cold northeaster was blowing through the town with the smell of coming snow on the wind. All day our house was hushed for a reason I didn't understand, and I remember being sent out to play with some other boys in the middle of the afternoon. Supper was a silent meal. And then, immediately after we had finished, my father put on the great-coat of his new uniform and went to the door and I saw the long tails of the coat blowing out behind him in the flicker of a faulty arc light as he half-ran up to the corner. We heard bagpipes, and almost immediately a company of soldiers appeared swinging down Spring Garden Road from old Dalhousie. It was very cold as we struggled up to the corner after my father, and he affected not to notice us. Then the pipes went by playing "The Blue Bonnets," the lines of khaki men went past in the darkness and my father fell in behind the last rank and faded off down the half-lit street, holding his head low against the wind to keep his flat military cap from blowing off, and my mother tried to hide her feelings by saying what a shame the cap didn't fit him properly. She told my sister and me how nice it was of the pipers to have turned out on such a cold day to see the men off, for pipe music was the only kind my father liked. It was all very informal. The men of that unit—almost entirely a local one—simply left their homes the way my father had done and joined the column and the column marched

26

down Spring Garden Road to the ship along the familiar route most of them had taken to church all their lives. An hour later we heard tugboat whistles and then the foghorn of the transport and we knew he was on his way. As my sister and I hung up our stockings on the mantelpiece I wondered whether the vessel was no farther out than Thrum Cap or whether it had already reached Sambro.

It was a bleak night for children to hang up their stockings and wait for Santa Claus, but next morning we found gifts in them as usual, including a golden orange in each toe. It was strange to think that the very night my father had left the house, a strange old man, remembering my sister and me, had come into it. We thought it was a sign of good luck.

That was 1915, and some time during the following year a boy at school told me there was no Santa Claus and put his case so convincingly that I believed him.

Strictly speaking, this should have been the moment of my first step toward becoming a neurotic. Maybe it was, but there were so many other circumstances to compete with it, I don't know whether Santa Claus was responsible for what I'm like now or not. For about a week after discovering the great deception I wondered how I could develop a line of conduct which would prevent my mother from finding out that I knew who filled our stockings on Christmas Eve. I hated to disappoint her in what I knew was a great pleasure. After a while I forgot all about it. Then, shortly before Christmas, a cable arrived saying that my father was on his way home. He hadn't been killed like the fathers of other boys at school; he was being invalided home as a result of excessive work as a surgeon in the hospital.

We had been living with my grandmother in Cape

Breton, so my mother rented a house in Halifax sight unseen, we got down there in time to meet his ship when it came in, and then we all went to the new house. This is the part of my story which reminds me of Charles Dickens again.   Five minutes after we entered the house it blew up.   This was not the famous Halifax explosion; we had to wait another year for that.   This was our own private explosion.   It smashed half the windows in the other houses along the block, it shook the ground like an earthquake and it was heard for a mile.

I have seen many queer accidents in Halifax, but none which gave the reporters more satisfaction than ours did.   For a house to blow up suddenly in our district was unusual, so the press felt some explanation was due the public.   Besides, it was nearly Christmas and local news was hard to find.   The moment the first telephone call reached the newspaper offices to report the accident, they knew the cause.   Gas had been leaking in our district for years and a few people had even complained about it.   In our house, gas had apparently backed in from the city mains, filling partitions between the walls and lying stagnant in the basement.   But this was the first time anyone could prove that gas had been leaking.   The afternoon paper gave the story.

DOCTOR HUNTS GAS LEAK WITH
BURNING MATCH—FINDS IT!

When my father was able to talk, which he couldn't do for several days because the skin had been burned off his hands and face, he denied the story about the match. According to modern theory this denial should have precipitated my second plunge toward neurosis, for I had distinctly seen him with the match in his hand, going down to the basement to look for the gas and complaining about how careless people were. However, those were ignorant times and I didn't realize I might get a neurosis. Instead of brooding and deciding to close my mind to reality from then on in order to preserve my belief in the veracity and faultlessness of my father, I wished to God he had been able to tell his story sooner and stick to it. After all, he was a first-class doctor, but what would prospective patients think if every time they heard his name they saw a picture of an absent-minded veteran looking for a gas leak in a dark basement with a lighted match?

It took two whole days for the newspaper account of our accident to settle. In the meantime the house was temporarily ruined, school children had denuded the chandelier in the living-room of its prisms, and it was almost Christmas. My sister was still away at school, so my mother, my father and I found ourselves in a single room in an old residential hotel on Barrington Street. I slept on a cot and they nursed their burns in a huge bed which opened out of the wall. The bed had a mirror on the bottom of it, and it was equipped with such a strong spring that it crashed into place in the wall whenever they got out of it. I still remember my father sitting up in it with one arm in a sling from the war, and his face and head in white bandages. He was philosophical about the situation, including the vagaries of the bed, for it was his Calvinistic way to permit himself to be comfortable only when things were going badly.

The hotel was crowded and our meals were brought to us by a boy called Chester, who lived in the basement near the kitchen. That was all I knew about Chester at first; he brought our meals, he went to school only occasionally, and his mother was ill in the basement.

But as long as my memory lasts, that Christmas of 1916 will be Chester's Christmas.

He was a waif of a boy. I never knew his last name, and wherever he is now, I'm certain he doesn't remember me. But for a time I can say without being sentimental that I loved him.

He was white-faced and thin, with lank hair on top of a head that broke back at right angles from a high narrow forehead. There were always holes in his black stockings, his handed-down pants were so badly cut that one leg was several inches longer than the other and there was a patch on the right seat of a different colour from the rest of the cloth. But he was proud of his clothes; prouder than anyone I've ever seen over a pair of pants. He explained that they were his father's and his father had worn them at sea.

For Chester, nobody was worth considering seriously unless he was a seaman. Instead of feeling envious of the people who lived upstairs in the hotel, he seemed to feel sorry for them because they never went to sea. He would look at the old ladies with the kind of eyes that Dickens discovered in children's faces in London: huge eyes as trusting as a bird-dog's, but old, as though they had forgotten how to cry long ago.

I wondered a lot about Chester—what kind of a room they had in the basement, where they ate, what his mother was like. But I was never allowed in the basement. Once I walked behind the hotel to see if I could look through the windows, but they were only six or eight inches above the ground and they were covered with snow. I gathered that Chester liked it down there because it was warm, and once he was down, nobody ever bothered him.

The days went past, heavy and grey and cold. Soon

it was the day before Christmas again, and I was still supposed to believe in Santa Claus. I found myself confronted by a double crisis.

I would have to hang up my stocking as usual, but how could my parents, who were still in bed, manage to fill it? And how would they feel when the next morning came and my stocking was still empty? This worry was overshadowed only by my concern for Chester.

On the afternoon of Christmas Eve he informed me that this year, for the first time in his life, Santa Claus was really going to remember him. "I never ett a real orange and you never did neether because you only get real oranges in Portugal. My old man says so. But Santy Claus is going to bring me one this year. That means the old man's still alive."

"Honest, Chester? How do you know?" Everyone in the hotel knew that his father, who was a quarter-master, was on a slow convoy to England.

"Mrs. Urquhart says so."

Everyone in the hotel also knew Mrs. Urquhart. She was a tiny old lady with a harsh voice who lived in the room opposite ours on the ground floor with her unmarried sister. Mrs. Urquhart wore a white lace cap and carried a cane. Both old ladies wore mourning, Mrs. Urquhart for two dead husbands, her sister for Queen Victoria. They were a trial to Chester because he had to carry hot tea upstairs for them every morning at seven.

"Mrs. Urquhart says if Santy Claus brings me real oranges it means he was talkin' to the old man and the old man told him I wanted one. And if Santy Claus was talkin' to the old man, it means the old man's alive, don't it?"

Much of this was beyond me until Chester explained further.

31

"Last time the old man was home I seed some oranges in a store window, but he wouldn't get me one because if he buys stuff in stores he can't go on being a seaman. To be a seaman you got to wash out your insides with rum every day and rum costs lots of money. Anyhow, store oranges ain't real."

"How do you know they aren't?"

"My old man says so. He's been in Portugal and he picks real ones off trees. That's where they come from. Not from stores. Only my old man and the people who live in Portugal has ever ett real oranges."

Someone called and Chester disappeared into the basement. An hour or so later, after we had eaten the supper he brought to us on a tray, my father told me to bring the wallet from the pocket of his uniform which was hanging in the cupboard. He gave me some small change and sent me to buy grapes for my mother at a corner fruit store. When I came back with the grapes I met Chester in the outer hall. His face was beaming and he was carrying a parcel wrapped in brown paper.

"Your old man give me a two-dollar bill," he said. "I got my old lady a Christmas present."

I asked him if it was medicine.

"She don't like medicine," he said. "When she's feelin' bad she wants rum."

When I got back to our room I didn't tell my father what Chester had done with his two dollars. I hung up my stocking on the old-fashioned mantelpiece, the lights were put out and I was told to go to sleep.

An old flickering arc light hung in the street almost directly in front of the hotel, and as I lay in the dark pretending to be asleep the ceiling seemed to be quivering, for the shutters fitted badly and the room could never be completely darkened. After a time I heard movement in the room, then saw a shadowy figure near the mantelpiece. I closed my eyes tight, heard the swish of tissue paper, then the sounds of someone getting back into bed. A fog horn, blowing in the harbour and heralding bad weather, was also audible.

After what seemed to me a long time I heard heavy breathing from the bed. I got up, crossed the room carefully and felt the stocking in the dark. My fingers closed on a round object in its toe. Well, I thought, one orange would be better than none.

In those days hardly any children wore pyjamas, at least not in Nova Scotia. And so a minute later, when I was sneaking down the dimly lit hall of the hotel in a white nightgown, heading for the basement stairs with the orange in my hand, I was a fairly conspicuous object. Just as I was putting my hand to the knob of the basement door I heard a tapping sound and ducked under the main stairs that led to the second floor of the hotel. The tapping came near, stopped, and I knew somebody was standing still, listening, only a few feet away.

A crisp voice said, "You naughty boy, come out of there."

I waited a moment and then moved into the hall. Mrs. Urquhart was standing before me in her black dress and white cap, one hand on the handle of her cane.

"You ought to be ashamed of yourself, at this hour of the night. Go back to your room at once!"

As I went back up the hall I was afraid the noise had wakened my father. The big door creaked as I opened it and looked up at the quivering maze of shadows on the ceiling. Somebody on the bed was snoring and it seemed to be all right. I slipped into my cot and waited for several minutes, then got up again and replaced the orange in the toe of the stocking and carefully put the other gifts on top of it. As soon as I reached my cot again I fell asleep with the sudden fatigue of children.

The room was full of light when I woke up; not sunlight but the grey luminosity of filtered light reflected off snow. My parents were sitting up in bed and Chester was standing inside the door with our breakfast. My father was trying to smile under his bandages and Chester had a grin so big it showed the gap in his front teeth. The moment I had been worrying about was finally here.

The first thing I must do was display enthusiasm for my parents' sake. I went to my stocking and emptied it on my cot while Chester watched me out of the corner of his eye. Last of all the orange rolled out.

"I bet it ain't real," Chester said.

My parents said nothing as he reached over and held it up to the light.

"No," he said. "It ain't real," and dropped it on the cot again. Then he put his hand into his pocket and with an effort managed to extract a medium-sized orange. "Look at mine," he said. "Look what it says right here."

On the skin of the orange, printed daintily with someone's pen, were the words, PRODUCE OF PORTUGAL.

"So my old man's been talkin' to Santy Claus, just like Mrs. Urquhart said."

There was never any further discussion in our family about whether Santa Claus was or was not real. Perhaps Mrs. Urquhart was the actual cause of my neurosis. I'm not a scientist, so I don't know.

3

ON DISCOVERING WHO
WE ARE

Throughout this collection there are several essays based more or less on the same theme. They form a pattern of my own growing consciousness of what it means to be a Canadian, but they are not set down in this book chronologically. Actually, this essay was my first public expression on the subject. Cross-Country *was the second.*

Comparisons may be odious, but it is only as we make them that individual identities become clear. For me, they have been necessary since the day I decided to root the scenes of my novels in Canada. It was then that I realized that I must first learn how to write a novel, true to its Canadian background, which would be at the same time intelligible and interesting to foreign readers, for a Canadian novelist cannot earn a living if he sells in the Canadian market alone.

The response to this article on the part of readers of Maclean's *surprised the editors as much as it did me. Apparently a great many Canadians are asking themselves the same questions I have been seeking to answer. Not the least of the wreckage left in the wake of the Second World War has been the torn fabric of our collective psychology. Gradually it has become obvious to most thinking Canadians that our relationships with Great Britain and the United States have undergone a rapid alteration. Canada today is in transition, and inevitably we are self-conscious. New definitions are required. It will do us no harm to repeat the questions more than once: What is a Canadian? What is our future rôle in the world? What emotions will our traditions stir in a crisis? What organic development is our country likely to have from here on?*

ON DISCOVERING WHO WE ARE

WHEN the difference between Canadians and Americans was first presented to me as the basis for an article, I believed it could not be done. For years I have known that Canadians and Americans, for all their surface resemblances, were different under the skin. Canadian mass-man differs noticeably from American mass-man. Yet the subject seemed too large and too vague to tie down with words, and the surface resemblances between Canada and the United States seemed too important.

Then one day not long ago I heard my neighbour's radio giving out a play-by-play account of the World Series, and I pictured men and boys in every city, town, village and farmhouse, in Canada as well as in the United States, sitting around their radios listening to that ball game.

An idea began to form and grow, so I walked down to the general store for cigarettes to think it over. On

37

the counter there I found eleven American magazines. Then I went over to the butcher's to get some lamb chops and found his radio on, so I sat on the counter with the butcher and smoked cigarettes and listened to the ball game myself.

No, I decided, you can't write an article on a subject like this. If you try, you'll only bog down in generalities and sound like a college professor talking over the CBC on Sunday afternoon.

Then another idea occurred to me. Suppose McGill were playing Western for the football championship of Canada. How many American radios would be tuned in on that game? Suppose I had walked into a general store in a village in Illinois. Would I have seen a copy of *Maclean's* or *Chatelaine* on the stands?

Here, I realized, was the most startling difference between Canada and the United States. Canadians read so many American magazines, listen to so many American programmes, see so many American movies, they can't help feeling themselves a part of American society. But they forget there is a twofold illusion in this feeling. The radio programmes and Hollywood movies give only a surface report on American life, or else they deliberately distort it. Moreover, this whole traffic in surface information runs south to north. Americans generally know nothing important about Canada, and care less.

When I reached home I decided that the job could be done, and that there was only one safe way to do it. I would tell about my own relations with Americans, and how I, personally, learned I was a Canadian. Such an approach will never qualify for a textbook on international relations, but it seems to me the only honest approach there is for a subject like this. In human affairs there is no absolute truth. Mainly, there is what a man finds out for himself, and this is coloured by his own personality and experience, it is transmuted by himself, it is shifted within himself whether he knows it consciously or not. I find I can't talk about the differences between Americans and Canadians without talking a good deal about myself.

In 1932, a few days after returning to Halifax from Oxford, I walked out to my old university to apply for a job. A vacancy had just been announced in my field of work, and in 1932 a new job of any kind was as rare as a snowball in August. This opening seemed to me one of those lucky chances which come rarely in life. My professors at the university must have had a fair opinion of my capacities, for it had largely been their recommendations which had sent me to Oxford as a Rhodes scholar.

But after talking for a few minutes with the professor who was then the head of my old department, I slowly became aware that he wished I had not come to see him.

Finally, he said: "You can apply for this job if you want to, but I may as well be frank. You won't get it."

I asked him why.

"An Englishman has sent in his application."

I said nothing. There had been plenty of Englishmen at Oxford far more able than I, and I would have been the first to admit it.

The professor then gave me the man's name and added, as a sort of afterthought, the class he had got in his Oxford Schools. I have never had a poker face, and in those days my face was open to the whole world. The professor smiled, for both he and I knew that the Englishman's class was exactly the same as my own. If academic qualifications were what counted, we were dead equals.

To this day I don't know whether the professor's next

39

remark was intended as irony, or whether it was merely the statement of a truth he thought I should accept as self-evident.

"After all, you're a Canadian and he's an Englishman. It makes a difference."

It was one of those arterial sentences. It went from my brain right through me till I felt it in the back of my legs.

The professor added, with sincere kindness: "You'd better drop the idea of teaching in Canada and go down to the States. A Canadian can always get a job there."

So, I thought, an old Tory in nineteenth-century England might have sat in his library facing his well-meaning but not too competent son, whom he had brought up with the idea that one day the ancestral land would be his, but now the ancestral land was mortgaged and a stranger was going to take it over.

"My dear boy, there's always the colonies. I don't know where they are myself, but your cousin Jasper had no more brains than you have, and they tell me that in Australia he's doing quite well."

As I walked home that day there was a warm westerly wind blowing. It had travelled all the way up the province, and the odours of the terrain it had crossed were still in it. I could smell spruce and salt water. At that moment all my instincts were against leaving this place. I felt I had been away long enough already. I had liked England. I can truly say I had loved Oxford, as a man loves any place which is greater than its temporary inhabitants. But Oxford was through with me now.

The professor's words recurred to me: "You're a Canadian. You should go to the United States." I realized that I had never before thought of myself as a Canadian.

For in Nova Scotia—and I have since learned that it is much the same everywhere in Canada—we were Nova Scotians first and Canadians only when we applied for jobs or passports, or when a war broke out and the Government wanted an army, and even then they said it was England, not Canada, that needed us.

I reached home and wrote applications for a job to every college and university in Canada. The only one reporting a vacancy was in the West. The head of the department wrote as follows:

"I will be glad to put your name and qualifications before the governors, but two Englishmen are applying for this job and I don't think you'll have much chance. American universities are always eager to have Canadians on their staffs. At present more than twenty presidents of American universities were born in Canada."

This professor lived nearly three thousand miles from Halifax. He had given me the same answer, springing from the same point of view, that in cultural matters an Englishman is *automatically* superior to a Canadian and that a Canadian is probably superior to an American. How astonished Americans would be at the latter part of this assumption I did not know then, but I know now that it would seem too unreal even to make them angry.

So that fall I enrolled in an American graduate college, which promised a student fellowship that would pay room, lodging and research tuition and nothing else. I sailed from Halifax on the old *Arabic* on a Friday in September, and reached New York thirty-six hours later.

41

It was on that vessel that I first encountered American mass-man.

The *Arabic* was crowded with tourists returning from a summer abroad, and the passenger list read like a roll call of the European nations between Lisbon and Riga. But they were all Americans, and they were going home. In spite of the differences in the pigments of their skins, the shapes of their heads, the tones of their voices, the varying amounts of money they had in the bank, they all seemed to share a common experience—the experience of being citizens of the United States—and when you observed them in the group you saw how it had marked them, as if they had all been in a war together. Individual Americans I had met before; many of them. For one year in Oxford I had shared a sitting-room with a man from Nebraska, one of the nicest and ablest men I have ever met. But on the *Arabic* I could see nothing but the group, and it was the most distinct thing of its kind I had ever encountered. I tried to understand what made it distinctive, for I felt the difference between it and me; I felt it as something physical, something terribly important, something bigger and more formidable than anything I had run into yet.

Before we reached New York I thought I had learned at least one thing. I was not sure of it then. It was so different from anything I had ever been told, I would have been afraid to repeat it. But after all these years I am not afraid to say it now, because for me, at least, it is true. The one group quality these people had which stood out above all others was hardness.

Americans in the group are harder than any body of Englishmen or Canadians I have ever seen, and much harder than the Italians I have seen milling in the streets of Milan on the occasion of some Fascist jamboree. It may be that in this respect Americans are like Russians, and that the size of the country and the vastness of the population have something to do with it. The hardness is not physical, but mental, and when they think as a group, when there is something which really moves them as a group, don't be misled by any signs of surface excitement or Barnum showmanship, for underneath the surface the group mind is as coldly impersonal as steel, and all the more effective because Americans do not know it is like this. They think themselves soft and easy-going as compared with other nations.

When the Japs bombed Pearl Harbor and the Germans followed it up with a declaration of war, I knew the Americans were going to be hard. All their righteous horror at the bombing of cities done by other nations would disappear. I knew they were going to bomb hell out of Germany and Japan, that they were going to wage war with loathing for its traditional aspects of infantry marches and travel in strange countries, but with a cold fascination for what they could do technically, and that engineers would work miracles now they had the government money behind them. I knew that the whole nation would come together and find itself, and in spite of the war be happier than it had been in the 1930's. I knew the Americans were going to display a ruthlessness—not crude, personal savagery hand to hand, but a mechanical and distant ruthlessness—which would make what Hitler and Tojo had in mind seem like something out of the Middle Ages. For the Americans, as a group, are the greatest military people the world has ever seen, because as a group they do not fight as soldiers. They fight as engineers, and they have reached the point now when it is only in wartime that the unique collective genius of their society can fully realize itself.

The *Arabic* had one more lesson to offer before she discharged us. When we reached New York an immigration officer came into the lounge in his brown uniform and tight American pants and a silver eagle on his cap. "American ceetizens dees a way." The sheep were parted from the goats. When my turn came with the foreigners to pass him, the lounge was almost empty and only a few of us were left. An Englishman next to me spoke.

"You know, if you asked that immigration man what part of Italy he came from he'd be insulted."

I wanted to know why.

"He's not proud of being born an Italian. He's proud of being an American."

Afterward I learned how true this was. The United States wipes out the European past of its citizens. But Canada seems to encourage all of us to remember where we came from in Europe. Fourth generation Canadians in Cape Breton can tell you the name of the Highland village from which their ancestors set out. I remember reading in a French-language paper, on the occasion of a by-election in Quebec, not only that General LaFleche was a sound *Canadien*, but that his ancestors before him had been sound too, having come from the cradle of French Canada, a particularly named region of Anjou.

The Canadian's sense of his European past is unique in North America. No Americans pride themselves on where their ancestors lived in Europe, or what they did there. Most of them don't even know.

After that first landfall in New York, I lived in the United States almost continuously for three years, in a university town in New Jersey where all the important college buildings except one were exact copies of famous structures in Oxford and Cambridge. But the resemblance was external only. Inside they were aseptic and modern, and what went on inside was not what went on in any English university.

In Canada the system of higher education is largely based on that of the Scottish universities. Superficially, American colleges resemble ours. But the attitude of their professors is very different, and what they value is different. The spiritual home of higher education in the United States, for at least a hundred years, has been Germany.

I have often thought that you need look no farther than this if you want to know why American universities, in spite of having a larger number of students proportionately than the universities of any other country, have so little effect on the thought and action of the United States as a whole. Americans wisely trust the football coach more than the professor, for the dry formalism of Heidelberg and Berlin seminaries does not fit the American mind, and Americans know it. So the university in the United States, when it is serious, is reduced to doing the only useful thing it can. It trains without educating. With the possible exceptions of Harvard and one or two other places, most of them small, hardly any American colleges raise students to think, and few of them even pretend to do so. Canadian colleges, at least until recently, *pretended* to teach their students to think for themselves.

But if there is a difference in the higher education of our two countries, the difference in the grammar schools and high schools is even greater and more influential. In American state-supported schools, nationalism is indoctrinated from the first grade. The American child pledges himself to his flag every morning. Up to the time of writing, Canada has no flag to which a child could pledge himself even if the politicians wanted him to do so. In the United States there are no separate state schools for religious denominations. In the United States the public school offers a dead level of uniformity from Boston to San Diego. Here the schools vary from province to province and even from town to town, and if the Federal Government tried to force an honest textbook for Canadian history on the schools of Quebec and Ontario, both provinces to use the same book, it would be voted out of office. The only uniformity which Canadian public schools offer is a uniformity in the wages they pay teachers. The average wage for a teacher in Canada is that of an unskilled, non-unionized day labourer.

Where two systems are bad, the only point in comparing them is to note the different directions in which the badness leads. American schools, as I said, foster nationalism; Canadian schools, provincialism. If the American system resembles Willow Run, ours is like a collection of old family businesses, some fairly good, others poor, others a disgrace to the community, nearly all of them paying sweated wages, and a large number of them borrowing from the bank every fall.

In my second year in the United States I bought a thirteen-year-old Studebaker which carried me, at a top speed of thirty-seven miles an hour, into every state north of the Mason-Dixon line between the Atlantic seaboard and Chicago. That Studebaker introduced me to Americans at their best, Americans on the road. I became acquainted with truck drivers, farmers, businessmen, travelling salesmen, hitchhiking unemployed, clerks leaving a girl in one town to go to a girl in another, bootleggers and bums.

Meeting them this way it was easy to know Americans

and impossible not to love them. This was how they seemed to themselves: on the road away from the business they are trained to pretend they like but seldom do. I had been thinking that Canada was a more real democracy than the United States; I still think it is, because we haven't as much wealth or as many factories. But on the roads democracy in the United States is very real, and you know that the country is greater than the factories which try to mechanize its feelings, and the advertisers who try to corrupt it, and the politicians and newspapers and movies that misrepresent it. If there is one thing for which I am grateful to the United States, it is for this sense of the open road. There is nothing like it in Canada. We haven't enough roads, and the ones we have are not wide enough or straight enough to give the feeling. Nor do we have wayside stopping places that make for good talk over good food.

In the United States nearly all the roads are wide, and they are more than a means of getting from one place to another. They stand for a way of life. They don't just lead from Chicago to St. Louis. They lead from Chicago, St. Louis, Detroit and Napoleon, Ohio, into the United States of legend, and they are among the things which make an American different from anyone else in the world. These great highways beckon the American to hopes that one in ten thousand fulfills; but the ten-thousandth man does it. They are the source of his freedom, just as they are also the source of his lawlessness. *Feelin' tomorrow just like I feels today—feelin' tomorrow just like I feels today—I'm gonna pack my bag and make my getaway.**

Only in the United States does the phrase, "get out

*The "St. Louis Blues," by W. C. Handy, with permission of Handy Bros. Music Co. Inc., copyright owners.

47

of town," mean what it does there. Only in a country with such an attitude toward roads could Matt, a sixty-year-old elevator man, making twenty a week in New York against rising prices, object to OPA as an infringement on his personal liberty. When I, down from Canada and proud of our price control, tried to argue that without OPA his wages wouldn't keep him alive, Matt's answer contained the reason for at least half of Harry Truman's headaches: "How do you know but what tomorrow may be my lucky day?"

Steadily, during those first three years in the United States, the knowledge was borne in on me that I did not fit. Except on the roads; anyone could fit there. It was all right drinking beer in taverns after work or eating hamburgers in diners and listening to the sagas of truck drivers, sometimes sitting on a barrel in the locked-up saloon on a Saturday night hearing the bootlegger tell about the ingratitude of human nature, how he had just smashed up the bar of his best friend with a pickaxe and sent his friend to hospital because the friend had hijacked his truck the previous Wednesday.

It was wonderful picking up the enormous variety of colour and excitement, considering the charm of women, their friendliness, the way they dressed and moved when they walked; sometimes going into New York on a week-end and observing, from the long distance of the sidewalk and the longer distance of only a few dollars in the pocket, the best-dressed women in the world stepping into taxis from the great hotels about the Plaza on their way to the theatre, while the sky over the park and Columbus Circle glowed with the last embers of sunset; and then the ramparts of the hotels along Central Park South breaking out their lights one by one until the whole was a cliff of light that finally lost itself in the purple upper darkness.

But the people here were not my people, nor could I easily become one of them. I missed the quietness of home. I missed the sense of my own past. I missed the knowledge that if I said something outrageous, people would not mark me down as queer, or automatically dislike me, but would make the allowances they will always make for a member of their own family, remembering that his background is also their background, and that the main part of a man is a product of it. A man needs a strange country to get a new sense of himself. But he needs his own country to be aware of his roots. Without using the phrase in the slightest sense nationalistically, I missed not being able to be a Canadian.

It was when I worked—and I did work most of the time—that I felt the widest difference. Then it was a matter of values: of things felt rather than of things said. The American attitude toward work is not quite the same as ours. They esteem work more, but they enjoy it less. On the whole there is less friendliness between co-workers; and where I was, there was more subservience to higher-ups. This subservience is, of course, not American; in their universities it derives from the German influence. But in all walks of life in the United States, the fierce American ambition to get along produces strain. Canadians view their jobs more as long-term propositions. Americans view them as stepping-stones to something better.

When you work with a people you must share their group values if you are to get along. If you don't share them, you must pretend that you do. Many Middle Europeans can pretend to share the group values of Americans better than a Canadian can, for the Canadian is so close to the United States that he often forgets that in American eyes he is a British subject. When he talks of how things are done at home, the American is apt to think he is criticizing, and no American can stand criticism from anyone who is British.

It took me a long time to accept the fact that in the eyes of the average American this whole continent—at least all of it that is worth much—belongs to him. Americans don't realize that Canadians have the same right to feel proprietary about it that they have themselves. An American does not see the point in our assertion that we have a right to find fault with an American government, or with American big business, because what is done by his government and his businessmen profoundly affects the well-being of all Canada. The American's superiority complex, when he thinks of his country, is greater than anything the world has ever seen. His answer to our comments would probably be this: "If you want to criticize us, become an American citizen before you talk."

For the American knows that people from all over the world have wanted to come to the United States. He has been far more generous with his country than we have been with ours, as the American foreign-born population testifies. But he wants people to feel grateful; grateful to the United States as a nation. He wants incomers to feel grateful for being in the United States. To a Canadian this is a strange point of view. We never expect an American to feel grateful to us just because he happens to be in Canada. He, like ourselves, is also a North American.

During that time in the university in New Jersey I made many mistakes in what was expected as conduct for an incomer. I grew increasingly uncomfortable. The head of my department, a wise and kindly man, finally said to me at the end of my third year, "Now you have your doctor's degree, I don't advise you to apply for a post in the United States. I say this for your own sake. You won't be happy here. I know your country, and I believe you will be happy there. Sometimes I feel I would fit better in Canada myself than I fit here. Canadians are what Americans used to be forty years ago."

But this professor was a very exceptional American. For an American to suggest that a man could do well in any country but the United States is so rare it is almost unthinkable.

A few months later, after all the training that was supposed to have given me so many advantages, I accepted a job in Montreal that paid me the wages of a petty clerk. I was glad of it at the time, and I'm not sorry I took it now. When I stepped off the train in the old Bonaventure Station, though I knew no word of French, I felt at home. In a French-Canadian village today, though my French is still not good, I can feel at home. And in Canada I have always felt at home in my work, which is the ultimate test.

The countless important things that matter are here understood. It is not necessary to act a part. I came back to Canada at a time when Canadians of my age, in all provinces, were discovering vaguely what the Canadian Army discovered positively during the war: a Canadian point of view, incoherent as yet but strongly felt, really exists.

This long account of how one man came to know he was a Canadian would never have been written if he had not married an American girl. It was she who helped me discover Canada, so that I could put some of it into words; for she, in her own way, found another framework of differences when she came to live in my country. It was she who showed me why the first two novels I had written were failures. I had set the scene and characters of one book in Europe, of the second in the United States. They were not authentic. The innumerable sense impressions, the feeling for country, the instinct for what is valuable in a human being—these things were all coloured by a Canadian background I had not accounted for, which neither an American nor a European would accept without an explanation that was an inherent part of the story. Few novelists, writing of contemporary life, can risk setting the scene outside their own country unless their country is known to the whole world, and unless they make one of their own countrymen the leading character. It was my wife who persuaded me to see Canada as it was and to write of it as I saw it.

So I have written and published two full-length novels with Canadian scenes, and now I am writing a third with scenes laid both in Canada and in the United States. Perhaps my life has made this third book inevitable. Ever since I returned to Canada I have been going back to the United States each year. Before the war we crossed the United States by car and lived for a while in California. We spent an entire winter in New York. In the summer we live in a Canadian village that was founded and is still dominated by Americans.

No good can come from the pretence that societies and nations do not differ from one another. Many differences between Canadians and Americans it will do us good to recognize. Canada is younger in time—in industrial time—than the United States. For the past hundred years social change has been almost entirely the product of science and technology. Industrialism in the United States is, by and large, fifty years older than it is here, in the sense that an industrial way of thinking, the application of mechanical principles to nearly everything, has penetrated American thought more deeply than it has ours.

The puritanism which is still dominant in Canada has grown so weak in most parts of the United States, particularly in cities of the East and in California, that you could almost think the coat had been turned inside out. The American divorce rate is now about ten times higher than ours. As a counterpart, there is more frankness between the sexes among Americans than there is here, especially among the middle-aged. Canadians are probably no more virtuous in thought than Americans are, but their inhibitions keep them from turning a good many of their ideas into action.

Americans are more optimistic, both about themselves and about their country, than Canadians are. The reason for this may be partly climatic, but most of it is historical. The United States was formed as the result of a successful revolution. Since that time it has never lost a war. Most of its great projects have been successful. But the original groups which developed Canada all became Canadians as the result of being on the losing side in war or revolution.

Americans are never afraid of making a mistake, and hold it against no one else if he does. This is the mark of a big man, and of a great nation. It is the reason the rest of the world admires them, in spite of their adolescence and lesser qualities. Canadians pay too much importance to mistakes. Our country is poorer than the United States, but we could make more of it than we do.

Americans are proud of what they do. The excessive

puritanism of Canadians makes them proud of what they don't do.

Americans think too large, and this makes them irresponsible as a nation. They are slow to realize how much bigger a portent the atomic bomb is than the miraculous engineering and scientific feats which produced it. But Canadians think too small, and this reduces our effectiveness as a nation. We let too many able men go to the United States because we are too small to give them what they need. Small thinking encourages mediocrity and denies greatness. Neither our large employers nor our Government has learned what all Americans take for granted: if you want the best, you must pay for it. If you want excellence, you must put up with its eccentricities and give it rein.

The Canadian and American attitude toward snobbery differs. In the United States a man is snobbish because he has too much money or because his family has been in the country a long time. In Canada money helps a snob as it does anywhere. But usually our snobbery is traceable to English ties, and certainly it does not depend on how long a family has been in the country.

Canada has a better form of government than the United States, and therefore a better ability to advance real democracy. The American Constitution is too rigid, and stays rigid because it has been made a sacred document. The chief executive in the United States has too much responsibility, because he is not supported by an elected Cabinet, and the pressure of work is too great for one man. Mackenzie King lasted for more than twenty years and improved with age like wine in the bottle. No American president could stay alive that long in office.

One thing I would like to say, which I hope any American who reads this will take in the spirit in which it is intended. I think that Canada has been, is, and may be in the future, more fortunate than the United States. We have never had a civil war, and therefore we have hardly any memories of mutual bloodshed. At the present time of transition, our small size of population makes the strains easier. In facing the future, we are less the prisoners of our own past. For it seems that nothing but catastrophe can check the furious progress of Americans into a still more bleak and dangerous desert of technology than they have reached now. The very vastness of the apparatus their genius has created stands over them now like a strange and terrible master. Every man, as Sophocles said years ago, loves what he has made himself. Canadians have as yet fallen in love with no such Frankenstein. And, as a result of this, our future is more clearly in our own hands. We are not so entirely in the grip of internal forces beyond our own control. Socialism in the United States, if it comes, might easily be totalitarian. Socialism in Canada, if it comes, will certainly be democratic.

We are fortunate, perhaps, because we are less rich in money. I do not intend this sentence as a text for a certain kind of employer who might use it as a pious pretext to underpay his labour. But the money in the United States is too big. Where money is the measure of too much, man is the measure of too little.

These many differences, of feeling and value, of fact and method, existing between the United States and Canada are all to the good. There are far too few differences on this continent as it is. The greatest spiritual enemy all North Americans face above the Rio Grande is uniformity. Industrialists and managers who measure life by production force more uniformity on us every year that passes. The economic man they were dreaming about a few decades ago would be, if he existed, nothing but an enormous consuming belly. The megalomania of technologists abets the managers in this. Those who would harness the power of the sun, who are plotting to control the weather by push buttons, are fools or hypocrites if they pretend that the attainment of such power in any near future would be anything but a monstrous evil. Mankind evolves slowly. Human society must be allowed to grow in its own time; like a tree, it should bear fruit in its season. Any gardener knows that you can only force the soil so far. If you do more than this, it rebels. If you give a plant too much chemical stimulant too quickly, it dies. The whole industrial process of this continent, like a ponderous animal which has not yet learned to reason, seems to feel by some primitive instinct that uniformity is desirable, that if all differences are wiped out between men, in effect only one man will be left. And, of course, it is easier to control one man than a multitude.

But these fears apply more to the future than to the present. At the present it is hard to see how Canada can become uniform, with the Province of Quebec in its heart. She can never, if we have the sense to see what she offers, be dull. She can never, with the United States beside her, be static. We have learned, both Canadians and Americans, something which no other pair of nations so mutually interdependent has yet learned in history. Real tolerance consists in much more than abstention in the use of military force to compel uniformity. It consists in the ability not only to recognize your neighbour's differences but also to enjoy them.

4

THE FACE OF POWER

I happened to pick up Yousuf Karsh's exhilarating book of portrait photographs, called Faces of Destiny, *the day after it was published. I leafed through it, put it down, bought another book I had entered the store to get, and left. Half-way down the block I turned about and went back to buy* Faces of Destiny *because I knew it would haunt me and nag at my mind if I didn't.*

I have yet to regret that unusually hasty decision, for I can still look at the faces in that collection and learn something. The book also gave me the pleasure of writing this article, which was exciting to me because in the process of doing it I learned something very important about modern history that I had not known before.

Many people, especially academicians, insist that it is impossible to tell anything about a man by looking at his face. As a novelist, I assert that such a statement is nonsense, and most policemen would agree with me. It takes some thought and considerable experience to learn what faces mean, to separate the individuality from the general. But once you embark on the study of faces, or the hobby, if you will, it is difficult to be dull for any length of time in a world so full of human beings.

I am sorry it is impossible to reproduce any of Karsh's photographs here, but the famous one of Winston Churchill—an embattled Churchill with hand on hip, no cigar for camouflage, underlip pouting, eyes remorselessly certain—is sufficiently well known by now to serve as an example of the manner in which this brilliant photographer of Ottawa has reproduced the men of power in this age.

THE FACE OF POWER

O F ALL contemporary artists the world over, the most likely candidate for immortality is the photographer Yousuf Karsh, Armenian-born Canadian citizen.

This statement is made in full knowledge that Picasso, Rouault, Henry Moore and other great artists are still alive. It is not made in the sense of comparing Karsh to them. It is not even sensible to compare the merits of a photographer to those of a painter. Quite apart from his capacity as an artist, which is great, the future fame of Yousuf Karsh will be fortified by the unique nature of his subjects. He has photographed, and revealed through the filter of his powerful brain, most of the men who guided the western nations to victory in the Second World War. When history reaches out for an understanding of these men it will use Karsh's portraits, for no one who sees these portraits can fail to be astonished by the nakedness of their veracity.

Great men rarely yield their secrets, especially if their greatness depends on the power they exercise over others. It is for this reason that statesmen and generals are seldom interesting. We are dazzled or frightened by the power they hold. We are painfully interested in what they do; what they do may kill us or save our lives. But we are seldom interested in them as real people, because they take good care to see to it that, as real people, we know nothing of consequence about them.

Portraits of kings, emperors and generals of past ages have one thing in common. Nearly all of them are dull. They tell us no more about their originals than Grant's Tomb tells us about General Grant. What do we learn of Queen Elizabeth by looking at the pictures of her? Merely that she had red hair, a thin face and wore too many clothes for the good of her health. Horatio Nelson was one of the most marvellously complex human beings who ever lived. But his monument in Trafalgar Square stands so high above the crowd that for all we know the face of a dustman may be underneath the pigeon-splashed, stone tricorne he wears. Recently there was a proposal to build a statue, on Dover Cliffs, of Winston Churchill wearing an admiral's hat and brandishing a cigar. If built, such a statue would have presented the war leader in his own carefully chosen disguise. Nobody knows better than Churchill himself that the cigars and the hats serve to humanize the elementally naked force compressed into his features.

Yousuf Karsh, with a gesture which has now become famous, took Churchill's cigar away from him before snapping the camera. As a result he shows us not merely the façade of power, but the unmasked expression of power itself. He shows us a man of controlled and frightening violence, a man of superhuman will and energy, an uncanny kind of intelligence which has marched far beyond the limits of cynicism, a man of so many parts that inevitably some portions of his nature are at war with others, yet withal a man whose face haunted Hitler before the war and drove him to despair during it.

This is the picture which made Karsh famous overnight. On the heels of its success he was sent to London to photograph the wartime great of Britain. On his return from London he was commissioned to make a series of portraits in Washington of American leaders and later to go to the United Nations Conference in San Francisco. Both before and after these special missions Karsh took many magnificent photographs of men less well known.

As Karsh himself reveals in his book, without saying so too specifically, the method he used with Churchill is the method he follows on every possible occasion. He removes the stage props, the carefully calculated gestures and expressions which great men use much as a conjurer employs byplay to conceal the real business of the act. Karsh goes straight to the point every time. He concentrates on the character harmony produced by the essential cast of features, by the essential look in the eyes, by the essential position of the hands. General Eisenhower, for instance, is presented without the famous grin. As a result, a pair of judging eyes stare out of a face as hard as steel, yet a face whose hardness we feel was necessary, because without it both he and the countries he served would have been lost.

In his book Karsh offers us twenty-six statesmen, three United States senators, ten generals, four admirals, the respective wartime chiefs of aviation in the British Empire and the United States, four royal personages, five famous businessmen who have also held public office, two publishers, six writers, one architect, one actor, two graphic artists, three diplomats (including Eleanor Roosevelt), two labour leaders, one scholar, one clergyman and one superdetective. The portrait of Mr. James McIntosh, chief messenger of the office of the Chief of Staff, United States Army, completes the total.

With only ten exceptions, Karsh's pictures are exactly what he claims them to be in the title of his book. They are faces of destiny. They are faces of men who like power, wield power, and above all, understand power. It is only when we examine his portrait gallery as a whole that we fully grasp the nature of his achievement. Karsh has revealed to us with naked clarity the kind of man who is supremely successful in our 'century.

The desire for power, the capacity to exercise it, have existed at all times. But the methods and manners of exerting power have varied according to the values, beliefs, superstitions, needs, capacities, knowledge and tensions of the times and places. The princely cardinals of Renaissance Italy, who compelled Galileo to announce publicly that the world did not revolve around the sun, did not resemble Karsh's subjects. The emotional, talkative, poetry-loving statesmen of Queen Elizabeth's era, revealed to us by Shakespeare and by their own writings, men who thought it no shame to weep in public, who faced a dangerous life with childlike zest and recklessness, would have been chilled and frustrated by the icy, close-lipped Cordell Hull. Self-confident, meat-eating Victorians, like Peel and Gladstone, would not have preserved for long their stolid belief in the inevitability of progress in a world where J. Edgar Hoover is necessary. Karsh has shown us that the face of power in the twentieth century is a very special kind of face. Indeed, one might almost call it a specialized face.

It is for this reason that Karsh, in my opinion, is sure of immortality. He has made an authentic and absolutely authoritative commentary on our age. Other artists in the past, Holbein, Van Dyck and Rodin, for instance, have painted or sculptured famous men. But none have made portraits of so many who are truly representative. By the time Karsh has finished his work he will very probably have rounded out his gallery by pictures of great scientists, engineers and industrialists. He will have photographed the majority of the men whose work, creative or administrative, makes our age uniquely what it is. A hundred years from now people will go to Karsh to see what dominant characteristics our age demanded in its leaders.

What will history think of them? All men judge others by the standards of their own background. We can only begin to guess what our descendants will think of us. But it is certain that we can understand better the nature and necessities of our own era if we take the time to assess the tone, character, possibilities and limitations of the men who have been studied by Yousuf Karsh.

For many years European thinkers have been telling us that the age we live in is decadent. For them, as Europeans, this may be true. But we in the British Commonwealth and the United States are no longer dominated by Europe, not even in the realm of ideas. The supreme attribute of decadence is weakness in the will. In a decadent society leaders are almost always capricious, unreliable and devoid of inner confidence. At their best they see too many sides of any public question to commit themselves to a single bold plan of action. They become like Hamlet, dissipating their force by too much speculation. At their worst they are cynical tyrants, irresponsibly and hysterically cruel, and they retain power because they surround themselves with men as vicious as themselves. Karsh shows us that whatever else our society may be, it is not decadent. Not yet.

The single quality which unites all of Karsh's men of action amid their many differences is the obvious fact that they have wills like steel. In nearly every one of his faces will power and logic completely dominate imagination. One looks—as Karsh makes us look—at Eisenhower, Admiral King, Cunningham, Churchill, Alanbrooke, Roosevelt, Marshall, Portal and Arnold. Then one thinks of the creatures they vanquished. Suddenly the Axis leaders seem amateurs of power compared to these men. Compared to Churchill and Roosevelt, Hitler was a screaming hysteric. Compared to Admirals Cunningham and King, Doenitz and Raeder were a pair of sour-minded, shifty little bureaucrats. Beside Portal, Milch looks like a circus showman. These men Karsh photographed lack many qualities. Not very many of them invite affection. But few of them lack the supreme quality necessary for a great leader. They have character. They have immense moral force.

Moral force, let us note, has nothing to do with whether a man is morally good or bad. It depends on a man's absolute inner conviction that he can carry through the job in hand without breaking under the strain, without losing his judgment, without becoming theatrical. It is quite as much a weapon as it is an attribute. In the past it has often rested on religion. Cromwell believed he was the Lord's agent and Glad-

64

stone thought he was God's mouthpiece. Abraham
Lincoln trusted humbly in Divine Guidance.

How many of Karsh's subjects derive their strength
from a deeply felt personal faith in God? Roosevelt did,
as we well know. W. L. Mackenzie King most certainly
does. King George does. Karsh had no opportunity to
make a real study of Roosevelt, but he reveals religious
faith in the eyes of the latter two men. Yet a close study
of most of these men of power leads one to believe that
their strength comes, not from reliance on a present
deity, but from a sure belief in their own integrity. By
integrity I mean nothing more than the inner strength
which prevents a man from betraying himself. The faith
of most of Karsh's subjects seems to derive from their
sureness that they have the know-how to win and the will
power to get the results they want.

These men are strained, isolated, specialized. They
are products of an age of exact science and massive
technical power. Many of them have been disillusioned.
They have learned, to their bitterness or satisfaction, that
such variables as human courage, faith, loyalty and
resolution are helpless against the blind and exact power
of machines. They have learned that, in an age of
science, time marches too fast to allow leisure for the
enjoyment of life, or even for the fruits of science itself,
if one also wishes to obtain power and hold mastery over
other men.

Not all of them, of course. By no means all of them.
And here lies still another excitement in Karsh's book.
It contains contrasts that are startling, brilliant and
sometimes poignant.

We see Lord Alanbrooke, who—we are told—more
than any other soldier, created the British Army after
Dunkirk. His picture follows that of Ernest Bevin. If

Bevin has the hardness of rough stone, this man has the toughness of polished steel. Looking at Alanbrooke's face, one knows that his purpose must be sane and intelligent. But once decided, nothing—absolutely nothing—would deflect him. One reads with initial surprise in Karsh's comment, which accompanies the picture, that Lord Alanbrooke likes birds. Then one is no longer surprised. Birds are high and lonely, too.

Consider the portraits of our two Canadian soldiers, General Crerar and General McNaughton. Then ask yourself why it was inevitable that Crerar superseded McNaughton. Karsh's pictures of the two men give at least one answer. Crerar's face and expression show that he belongs fully to this century. It is a "specialized" face. The sharp eyes focus directly on a single point. One hand lightly grips the wrist of the other. Crerar is concentrated. His will seems canalized. McNaughton, on the contrary, seems to know almost too much, he is proud and acquainted with doubt. His scientific imagination chafes at the monastic limits imposed by the necessities of military power. Is this what Karsh sensed when he showed him peering into the higher, unseen distance, his tense hands clutching and wrinkling the chest pockets of his uniform?

Of all these faces, the one which seems to me to reflect the distilled essence of the spirit of our time is that of J. Edgar Hoover, the leader of the G-Men. Here is a terrific concentration of relentless, nervous, lonely ability harnessed to a single purpose by a will so strong one wonders how his tense body manages to contain it. Here is a man who knows that to enforce the law in the modern industrialized United States one must be as precise, efficient, merciless and unreflective as a machine. Surely Hoover is a man for whom nothing counts but results. His stubby fingers lock into each other like the jaws of a bear trap. God help the criminal who crosses him. He will think further, act faster, and strike harder than any of them would dream of doing.

How do the idealists appear among Karsh's subjects?

Sir Stafford Cripps is uneasy. He looks at us like a brilliantly clever student sitting on tacks waiting to give answers to a group of professors who, he believes, have always underrated him and who will, in any case, lack the intelligence to know what he is talking about.

Henry Wallace is a man in middle life, but in spite of the greyness in the hair and the crow's-feet about the eyes, he still seems young. No appetite or aptitude for power shows in his sensitive hands; they might belong to a surgeon. He reminds one of an intense and well-thought-of senior in a denominational college in the American Middle West, a lad who has made himself respected even by the loafers and poker players, has been president of various student societies, and finally has been appointed valedictorian of his class. As Karsh shows him to us, he might even be the leader of the debating team. He has mastered all the arguments. His side is right. But will the judges be fair? He seems to be regretting that older people do not possess the simple common sense of youth. Also there are rogues in the world. They listened to Lincoln. Why not to him? Meanwhile the debate must still be won. After that there will be many more debates. Even a lifetime of debating may be necessary, but ultimately the truth, like murder, will out. Is this why Henry Wallace takes his place among the close-lipped, hard-handed men who have learned that in their business personal friends are luxuries?

Clement Attlee, by a beautiful touch of symbolism on

the part of the photographer, holds a copy of a San Francisco newspaper in his hand and smiles his good will at the whole world. We like Attlee. Here is a man who knows the score and has chosen the weaker team because the weaker team needs him. Human beings come no better than this man.

Sir William Beveridge, at first glance, seems to be smiling. Then we suddenly realize that his lips are closed, his eyes are rather grim, and the thumbs of his bony hands are hooked into the lower pockets of his waistcoat. He has been a teacher. He knows how hard it is for stupid people to get the point. "There you are!" he seems to be thinking. "I've showed you how to do it. I've showed you perfectly clearly, and now you very probably will go off and act just as stupidly as you always do." There is knowledge in the eyes of Sir William Beveridge. He has no illusions about a world containing the Hoovers, the Alanbrookes, the Beaverbrooks and the Molotovs. He knows that the furious passions and inner conflicts Karsh has revealed in the face of John L. Lewis will not be eager to advance the cause of labour by the peaceful methods he advocates. A pure idealist might be defined as a man who is positive that other men, with equal knowledge, will be as reasonable as himself. A pure cynic is a man who is positive that nobody, not even himself, can ever be reasonable at all. Sir William Beveridge is obviously no cynic. But from the picture Karsh has taken of him one is justified in assuming that he is only a moderate idealist.

We pass on to H. G. Wells. No writer of our century wielded a greater influence than did Wells in his prime, nor was any other so self-confident. He sincerely believed that men, if educated to a better course, would be sure to follow it. He was confident that material progress would usher in the millennium. In book after book he attacked the old religious concept of life. Science became his god. He was opposed in principle to the humanities in education. He was sure that science would make us wise, and that wisdom would make us kind.

Karsh shows us an older and sadder Wells. The eyes are almost closed. Light as from a church window strikes his forehead. His hands are clasped as if in prayer before an altar. Shortly after this picture was taken Wells published his last book. It was called *Mind at the End of Its Tether*.

Among these portraits of modern men appear several of aristocrats who, in spirit and training, belong to an earlier and more urbane age. Notable among them are Henry Stimson and former Chief Justice Charles Evans Hughes. It is interesting to note that the two most aristocratic-looking men in the whole collection are Americans. But the difference visible in their expressions is startling.

Chief Justice Hughes had the air of a man who knew he no longer belonged to our time and was on the whole thankful he didn't. Noble, good-humoured, magnificent, he retired from public life in 1941. He sat to Karsh like an ancient patriarch who knew his work was done. When the sitting was finished he said: "Now lettest thou thy servant depart in peace." We look at him and feel envious. The times which moulded him were kindlier than our own, and they also had more savour.

Henry Stimson, on the other hand, is a man of Hughes' own vintage who, with the fidelity of an ancient republican Roman, served his country until the Second World War was won. By a strange irony it was Stimson, perhaps the most civilized man in the United States Government, who had to recommend that the atomic bombs be dropped on Japan. With typical integrity he has made no secret of his share in this terrible act. Sad, humble, resolute, his old eyes have seen hope after hope rise like a mirage and melt away. He has seen Bismarck replaced by the Kaiser and the Kaiser by Hitler. He has witnessed, helplessly, the weak complacency of President Hoover and Prime Minister Baldwin in the face of Japan's disregard of treaties. He has been forced to temper his own inner gentleness to the iron he saw confronting him. How strange it is that the two gentlest faces in the whole Karsh collection should belong to Henry Stimson, Secretary of State for War, and General Marshall, Chief of Staff of the United States Army! Both these men are like Romans of the great period of Roman character.

Roman also are Lord Wavell and Sumner Welles. Wavell, though only nine years senior to Welles, seems to belong to an older generation. He is more rugged. He is not drawn so fine. But both of these men, each with his own emotions, could have sat in the Roman senate after Cannae and, with Hannibal at the gate and no new army obtainable for years, have voted to resist to the end. In a superb picture Welles stands with folded arms before a closed door, straight, slim and upright, looking into your eyes.

It is inevitable that one should think of Rome when one studies this book of Yousuf Karsh. The only portraits of public men which can be compared to these in any sense are the great portrait busts of the ancients. The lines in the face of Julius Caesar are the same lines we find in the face of Lord Alanbrooke. The nameless sculptor who put Augustus on his monument has shown to twenty centuries the icy coldness of that dictator's solitude. Augustus and Cordell Hull could have understood each other by the exchange of a single glance.

And why not? The Romans of the period of the first two Caesars were men very much like ourselves. They had lived through a period of civil war and class violence. Their entire economic system was disorganized. They had fought a whole cycle of foreign wars, and, as a result of their victories, found themselves saddled with the responsibility of many nations besides their own. On one side of them were dying cultures, on the other were cultures struggling to be born. The brute force of barbarism lurked in the forests across the Rhine and the Danube. Like us, these Romans lived in a period of decaying faith and superlative advances in organizational and engineering skill. Like us, they came to believe that it is only through centralized control, exercised by a vast apparatus of state, that men can be governed efficiently. Like us, they had character, but character strained to the breaking point by violent experiences. Also like us, they had faith in little beyond their own abilities. Can we hazard a guess what the future holds, after comparing these men of our own time with the Romans?

Under the first Roman emperor, all for a time went well. Peace was established and enforced. The known world was policed by troops. Economic reorganization vastly increased the world's wealth. Even the poets of Rome seemed delighted by the superior organization and concentrated power their leaders had given their nation. Then, with the second emperor, people looked around them and felt that life was beginning to lose its savour. Very rapidly after this the inevitable decadence set in.

Walk through the great hall of the Uffizi Gallery in

Florence, or obtain from your public library a copy of a book containing the portrait busts of the emperors of the decadence. Stop before the bust of Nero and look well, remembering as you do that under him the Empire was prosperous for many years. It was a genius who revealed in polished stone the oyster-soft, neurotic cruelty of Nero's character. Walk a few steps farther down the hall and stop before the wrinkled forehead of Caracalla. Here has been engraved every infirmity of supreme power without ability, of supreme authority without morals: low cunning, suspicion so all-embracing it defeats its own ends, cynicism, inner terror, hatred, and the kind of cruelty which strikes blindly to destroy—without intelligence—whatever its haunted imagination dreads. How did a sculptor manage to reveal such things about a tyrant and live? Within the stone of the head itself posterity has the answer. Caracalla was stupid. He was too insensate to understand that the slave artist, whom he confronted in his toga, saw through its purple to the nakedness of the man within.

Fortunately for us who are now alive, the men Karsh portrays are not men of decadence. Nor does it necessarily follow that, after the present iron age, the overstrained character is sure to break and a decline set in, though history, for what it may be worth, points inexorably in that direction. Perhaps, for the time being, it is just as well to be content with what Karsh has to tell us about the nature of power in the western world today.

Two thoughtful men, Lord Acton and Henry Adams, have each uttered famous statements on the nature of power.

Lord Acton said: "Power corrupts, and absolute power corrupts absolutely. All great men are bad."

Henry Adams said: "Power is poison." Accepted superficially, as it usually is, this is the statement of a man disgusted by what he has seen of public life. But if we think about it more carefully, we realize that the statement is essentially tragic, whether Adams intended it to be so or not.

Somebody must assume the burden of power if organized society is to exist. Power issues its own rules. It is a separate world. It creates its own climate. To wield power with integrity, a man must accept a sort of poison within his veins. He can afford few friends among his equals lest it become his public duty to betray them. He can afford few luxuries lest he soften his purpose. He must starve his spirit lest his imagination revolt against the narrowness of the life he leads. In fighting against villains he must often use the methods of a villain, and be prepared to take advantage of fear, shame, hatred, vanity and ambition in the men with whom he inevitably must deal. In guarding civilization he must on occasion act like a savage.

With few exceptions, the subjects of Yousuf Karsh come under this latter definition of power. However much they may differ in capacities and aims, they have this one thing in common. They are tense, lonely men, controlling the destinies of a tense, lonely age.

5

CROSS-COUNTRY

There is only one point to remember when this essay is read: it was written in January, 1948, while almost every country in the world was looking at the United States in a mixed spirit of hope, frustration and despair. The prolonged debate on the question of the Marshall Plan had taken a discouraging turn. Isolationism seemed to be growing, and everywhere echoed the whispers which said that military men in Washington were thinking in terms of an American Empire. While Communists gained steadily in Europe and Asia, a Republican Congress—in spite of the efforts of such Republicans as Senator Vandenberg—seemed determined to play politics with destiny in order to confound a Democratic president.

To me it is a matter of humility as well as of encouragement to read this piece nearly two years after it was written and find how much I overrated the influence of Henry Ford in modern American life. Ford's values and principles are still influential in everyday habits and in educational techniques, but whenever a truly great issue is put before the Americans, the tradition of Jefferson means more to them than the shibboleths of efficiency experts. In their acceptance of the Marshall Plan, in the spirit in which they signed the Atlantic Pact, Americans proved themselves capable of rising to meet an unprecedented challenge in international affairs and of doing so within the compass of their Constitution.

CROSS-COUNTRY

THE entire world is asking itself what the United States, faced by the greatest challenge history has offered any nation, is going to do. The questions are simple and brutally urgent.

Is the United States still isolationist at heart? Is she going to be the first world citizen, a new species of international leader? Or is she going to put her ultimate faith in her technical and military skill and join the large company of imperial failures who have conceived it their duty to impose their ideas on everyone else by economic or military force?

None of these questions can be answered by reading the newspapers or by talking to politicians in Washington. If they could be, the rest of us would know where we stand. If they could be, I would have been far less eager than I was last autumn at the prospect of crossing the United States by car and I would have learned far less than I did on the journey.

Like everyone else, I have made my share of generalizations about the United States and, like everyone else on the outside, I have tended to consider only a part of the country, mainly the eastern seaboard and the Middle West, the sections where I have lived for months at a time and at two periods in my life for a matter of several years. It was nearly nine years since I had been through the hinterland. Though I firmly believed, and still do, that the final meaning of American life reveals itself most clearly and in greatest variety in the cities of the East, I still remembered that Americans put an almost superstitious faith in the vigour and purifying breezes which sweep across the grass roots.

It was the first week in December when Dorothy and I left Montreal. We reached California three weeks later and have been here ever since. During that time I have acquired an assorted kind of information which would sound impressive if I could quote what this or that important man in this or that key state told me. But I know few important men west of Philadelphia and the majority of the people I talked to were the sort Henry Wallace believes he compliments when he calls them common men. I have also studied with some care a variety of local newspapers from Rochester, N.Y., to Phoenix, Ariz. I have made a habit of listening to a great many radio programmes we never hear in Canada. So my fact-finding equipment has consisted of nothing but two eyes and a pair of ears and that indefinable sense of other people, highly personal and often unreliable, which all novelists learn to depend on in their work. My conclusions are therefore personal, necessarily coloured by my own interests and temperament.

We have seldom set out on a trip in a more peaceful state of mind. Dorothy had been exceedingly ill and months ago she had been ordered to a warm climate this winter by her doctor. In the language of the Foreign Exchange Control Board, "one consort" was given permission to accompany her out of the country and that took care of me.

We drove through northern New York, rounded the grey and dirty bend in the lakes to Cleveland, and the third day sliced off the northern part of Ohio and Indiana on the road to Chicago.

On the North Shore of Chicago we know many people, for it was there that we were married. I remember Chicago best in the splendid days of prohibition when Chicagoans justified their indifference to the local gang shootings on grounds of economy: it saved police expense to let the gangsters wipe each other out. I remember it in the winter of 1932 when the unemployed slept wrapped in newspapers under conduits and on the ledges above the urinals in men's lavatories in railroad stations. Now Chicago is on top again and you can smell its prosperity in the factory smoke which lies like a brownish-grey roof over Whiting, Calumet, East Chicago, Gary, Hammond and much of the South Side.

At this point I enter dangerous ground. The Middle West is a subject which outsiders approach at their peril.

If this section of the United States is not the brain of the country, it is certainly its heart, and the great muscle by which the vitality of that heart is generally measured is Chicago, together with its contingent suburbs known by group names. The heart is not a particularly complex organ. Unless it is diseased one lives for years without being conscious of it. It is less sensitive than the eye or the ear, it is far less mysterious than the brain. But since it is the one organ without which

79

none of the others can live, even the jokes we make about it are tinged with a certain grim seriousness.

This peculiar importance of the Middle West cannot be overemphasized. Because it is the heart of the United States, the Middle West comes close to being the heart of western civilization. That is why Sinclair Lewis, after spending a profitable lifetime lampooning it, still seems to consider it the only part of the earth's surface which really matters. That is also why the *Chicago Tribune*, even if it is not the world's greatest newspaper as it claims to be, shares with *Pravda* the distinction of being the world's most important newspaper. As *Pravda* is the trumpet of Russian nationalism, so the *Tribune* is the trumpet of American nationalism. As *Pravda* claims to speak for the proletariat, so the *Tribune* claims to speak for the middle classes.

The Middle West is the last great fortress of the middle class. In spite of the growth of labour unions, the tone, style, thought and values of the heart of America is still determined by the middle class. And broadly speaking, because the prosperous middle classes of the Northern United States stem directly out of the puritan movement, this means the dominating point of view in the Middle West is puritanism. Whether midwesterners go to church on Sundays or stay at home to read the comics in steam-heated apartments makes no difference, for puritanism is a state of mind no more fundamental to religion than a coat of barnacles is fundamental to the keel of a ship. Their manners may be easier than those of their ancestors, their prosperity may be Roman by comparison. The old morality based on sex may have yielded to the new morality based on what they call the American Way of Life, but its dynamics remain the same.

The middle classes of this part of the United States have the strengths and weaknesses of puritans everywhere. They are tremendously industrious, competent, hard-headed, practical and courageous. On the other hand, they understand internal-combustion engines better than they understand themselves, and they trust efficient organization more than they trust human nature. Nothing mysterious appeals to them or seems important. That is why they have no sense of history, which is a very mysterious process. Though they may pity weakness in others, they can never respect it. Though they dread failure, they tend to feel it is self-deserved. Though they are quick to criticize others, they have usually been so sharply handled in youth that they lose judgment when they are criticized in turn. Puritans everywhere find it necessary to maintain their sense of balance by active hostility to any morality which differs from their own. This is a statement which needs no enlargement in Canada, for the historical attitude of Ontario to Quebec is a living proof of its truth.

Practically every aspect of the attitude and behaviour of the Middle West in our century becomes crystal-clear the moment one realizes that it is the attitude of a puritan to what he considers a wicked world. Implicit in their conversation nowadays is the belief that if Europeans had modelled themselves on the Middle West, instead of giving themselves over to cussedness, they could have been prosperous, too.

America's crisis, and therefore the crisis of the rest of us, consists in this: puritanism has conditioned its members to act rather than to think, to deal with means rather than with ends, to press forward with ever-increasing speed and efficiency toward a material goal. Today, after having advanced further into a materialistic

paradise than any other people, Americans find themselves staring over the edge of a precipice, unable to
make up their minds where to go.

We met old friends in and around Chicago and no
people could have been more charming or friendly than
they were. Perhaps because I was a Canadian, more
probably because they were kindly individuals, all of
them at one time or another contrived to apologize for
the *Tribune*, which in two issues that week-end contained
an offensive article on England and a passing sneer at
Canada. Yet, in spite of these apologies, the course of
conversation through several evenings taught me the
truth of one thing Dorothy has always insisted I should
remember when I consider the Middle West. Most of
the political ideas uttered in this area are not original
with the people who express them. They can nearly
always be traced, however indirectly, to the *Chicago
Tribune*.

One man I met favoured giving aid to western Germany at the expense of Britain and France because—so he
believed—the British were Socialists and the French were
Communists. Because German settlers in the United
States had always worked hard, he drew the conclusion
that the Germans in the Reich were a sound people. He
insisted that the British were far less hungry than the
Government in Washington said they were and even if
they *were* hungry he considered it to be their own fault
because the British, as a people, were lazy. The French,
he said, were corrupt.

Another man (and these were all university graduates,
most of them trained in professions) admitted that he
held no brief for the Nazis; the Nazis were as bad as
anyone could possibly be. But he felt no inclination to
hold the German people responsible for Hitler. "Look

at us," he said. "We had a dictator in our own country from 1932 to 1945. Hitler may have started the war in Europe, but we'd never have gone to war with Japan if it hadn't been for Roosevelt."

Once upon a time I would have become enraged by such statements. Now I realize that when puritans talk like this they are merely relieving an accumulation of pressures within themselves. Foreigners are wrong if they believe such remarks prove these people to be men of ill will.

There are thousands of important things which I could say about the reservoir of good in the Middle West, but my purpose here is to try to understand how this area will affect the rôle of the United States in the future, and that question must override my desire to paint the other side of the picture. There is much that is beautiful in the Middle West, but it is not the dominant factor in the thinking of the people who live there, for they consider usefulness a higher virtue than beauty. It is a view with which most Canadians would agree.

Harold Stassen says that the Middle West is no longer isolationist. Very possibly the young men returned from the war have made it less so than it was in 1940. But it was my impression that it would take a violent shock to awaken the people here to any real sense of the jeopardy in which the world stands, or to the part which they themselves are going to be called upon to play in the future, whether they want to or not.

It was cold as we drove south, though we were well out of the range of snow. It was still cold as far south as Mississippi. The sky was heavily overcast and a wind that had started in the vicinity of Hudson Bay felt like the pressure of a cold hand fretting naked skin. Among brown cotton-fields, in shanties without heat and without water, Negroes were living with their chickens and half-starved mules. There were no dark-skinned mammies with heads tied in red bandannas picking cotton, but otherwise it was like every book ever written about this state. Southerners tell us one must live and grow up there to understand the reasons for its poverty, for Jim Crow and all the rest of it. They may be right. For us, merely driving through, it was a major experience which we found it difficult to believe.

We stopped for lunch at the best hotel in a medium-sized town somewhere in the middle of the state. There was nothing wrong with the town except the expressions on the faces of everyone in the place. We were depressed by the sights of the day, but they seemed depressed by their whole lives.

In the afternoon we stopped at a crossroads country store. Freshly slaughtered hogs were being carried into a shed at the back. Around a cracked stove in the middle of the one room sat six or seven pitch-black elderly Negroes, huddled together for comfort as much as for warmth. The two or three white men in the store were behind the counters, all with pinched, lean faces. When they talked to one another or to us they spoke in slow, courteous voices. But all over the room there was the smell of fear—fear of a different kind from the mental chimeras which plague the dreams of the puritans to the north. Here it was real. It was a part of the landscape, part of the rib-showing cattle grazing on brown earth, part of the knowledge that every man in the room—every man in that part of the country—was economically the enemy of every other man. To be sure, Mississippi is only a portion of the South. Having seen it, one can know there is nothing worse in the United States. But one can also know why hatreds and fears in this particular state leave no room for consideration of the wider issues of foreign affairs.

We dropped farther south and it was still cold. We passed through Vicksburg, and Natchez with its wonderfully beautiful, cold and useless mansions, and down the Natchez Trace to Baton Rouge, where we spent a night.

If I turn this into a travelogue I will be getting away from my point, but I learned long ago when I was travelling in Russia that without some feeling of the country where you find them, ideas seldom mean much. As an example, I can describe how we drove from Baton Rouge to New Orleans along a modern concrete road that has been built high over swamps which are a jungle of twisted, half-dead trees, water hyacinths and Spanish moss, passing every now and then shacks built on stilts over the swamp, shacks lived in by people who earn their living there. Every mile or so we saw a drowned steer floating upside down in the swamps beside the road. They were apparently animals that had been let out to graze on the Government-kept parkway beside the road, had wandered into what looked like another green lawn and had sunk down into the ooze beneath the carpet of water hyacinths. In the summer these swamps are infested with moccasins and malaria-carrying mosquitoes and they steam in the heat. How many people find the will to drive miles in order to vote on a hot day in a country like this? How can any of these people, themselves desperately poor, be concerned with what happens to the poor in Europe?

And yet for all its bad name, the South as a whole has a wisdom the North has never learned. During the past year I have been in every state in the South with the exception of Alabama, and I have reached a conclusion which is a paradox only on the surface. In one

85

sense, the South is the least isolationist part of the United States. I have heard half a dozen men in different states, poor men who worked with their hands, speak more intelligently about America's part in the world today than any of their counterparts in the Middle West. From their own poverty they have learned how people act when they are hungry. From their own sins they have learned what hatred—the kind that lets blood—will cause men to do. From their defeat in the Civil War they know what an invading army on the soil of its native land will do to a people's soul.

The South does not want to be defeated again. It has been solid behind all army appropriations. The southerner knows that a poor man has value and in his eyes the materialistic panacea of the puritans in the North is without prestige. Naturally, his poverty being what it is, his local politics resemble a quagmire and some of his politicians, such as the late Senator Bilbo, behave in public like denizens of the swamp. Yet I think it no accident that Woodrow Wilson came from North Carolina and Virginia, that Cordell Hull is a native of Tennessee, and that James Byrnes, General Marshall and that eminently influential figure in current American foreign policy—Bernard Baruch—are all southerners.

Such considerations aside, the delta country of Louisiana looked ominous and we found it a relief to head west into Texas after three days in New Orleans.

All the small towns of Texas appear to have happened recently and none of them seems to expect to stay as it now is for long. In places like Luling, Hondo and Uvalde the streets are laid out wider than the widest boulevards in Montreal and over them all there is an endless stretch of deep-blue sky. Texans have always thought of themselves as a unique race of men, as they *are* when the qualification rests upon the place in which they live. Besides the ranges and the cattle on them, there is the oil, and besides the oil there are huge sectional farms. From the mammoth storage tanks and chemical plants of Texas City across the bay from Galveston, to Randolph Field which trains fliers, to the King Ranch which raises cattle and race horses, there is nothing anywhere else in the world comparable for size. Imagination is stunted merely by looking at the imponderable dimensions of them. Even the men in Texas are, on the average, the biggest I have ever seen. They are big all over, with muscular faces, wide features, large powerful behinds and big hands. They walk and talk with a superb confidence and a charming courtesy. What can be more ingratiating than a huge, tough-looking man who speaks with a smile and a soft, southern accent?

This is a state which one would naturally look to as an active force for American leadership in the world, as a seed-bed for the creative ideas people are so desperately asking of the United States. Yet Texas must be counted out, unless you can give me a few names I've overlooked. One of its senators is Tom Connolly, an old-line party politician. The other is Pappy O'Daniel, perhaps the most completely irresponsible man in American public life. Only a week ago I heard him say over the radio that Washington is a gambling hell, that Europe has plenty of money to buy food in the "good old American way" and that the Marshall Plan is a deliberate plot formed by New Dealers to ruin the economy of the United States.

Why does a state as fine as Texas send a man like Pappy O'Daniel to Washington to represent its people? I don't know, unless the majority of the voters are too busy out there on the ranges, living in their marvellous climate, thinking about millions of head of cattle and new oil wells coming in every day, to give a damn about politics. They are still expanding a frontier and it appears to consume all the time and energy they have.

After a thousand miles of driving across Texas we crossed into New Mexico and southern Arizona, a world where nature has gone surrealistic. Mountains rise blue on the horizon above a yellow and copper-coloured desert, not only in ranges but also in lumpy forms that resemble parts of the human body, and everywhere colours are wild and glorious. The warm sun beats down steadily and only the strange organ-pipe cactus casts a thin line of shadow that could hardly be called shade. There are copper and silver mining towns like Globe and Miami, reached through canyons whose convoluted walls vary from mustard-yellow to rich red, and there are flat towns like modern caravansaries, each with its sun-baked motel.

No one you meet in New Mexico or Arizona seems to belong there; everyone has come from some other part of the country to sit in the sun. Yet it was New Mexico that gave the soldiers of the American Army its two finest spokesmen. Ernie Pyle was killed in the Pacific, but Bill Mauldin came home to record the life of a young man during these last two years in America with more wisdom, wit and fundamental intelligence than anyone else who writes books today.

When I was in England in 1932 the dead hands of Ramsay MacDonald, Stanley Baldwin and Neville Chamberlain were gripping the country and I heard the young men of Britain say that the next decade was going to be a race between themselves and the old men who ran it still. It was not wild talk. As history proved, it turned out to be an accurate prophecy, though the young men needed then, as they do now, a man of experience like Churchill to lead them. When I think of Bill Mauldin and millions of other young Americans like him, I can believe that the experience of the young men of England is repeating itself. In Britain the cleavage between the older and younger generation now seems to be healed. In Canada it is less apparent than it was ten years ago. But in the United States it has widened to a chasm and no appraisal of America's part in the future has any validity unless this cleavage is taken into account. Young men all over the country are as much disgusted with the two older political parties as Mauldin is. It is a tragedy that so many of them, lacking his perceptions, have found no better alternative than Henry Wallace.

Four hundred miles of driving remained for us between Phoenix and the Pacific coast. We found our way down into the Imperial Valley by a passage which must have been terrible even as recently as forty years ago, for most of the valley is below sea level and the mountains that frame it on both sides have been scorched almost bare of vegetation. In summer the noontide heat tops 120 degrees in the shade, and during this winter the valley has been suffering night temperatures of twelve degrees of frost.

At Indio we passed through miles of date orchards that reminded me of old-fashioned pictures from the Bible, and then the citrus groves began, miles and miles of oranges and grapefruit and lemons shining in the sun.

There are few parts of the world better calculated to give one renewed faith in mankind than this part of southern California, for it is a country which man, not God, has rendered habitable. As you pass through little

89

towns which had no existence ten years ago, white-walled and tile-roofed, you hear the whisper of sprayers on the lawns and see flaming branches of bougainvillaea dripping over trellises, and flowers which are nameless in your own vocabulary blooming in dooryards, and everything seems supremely right and good, for most of this development is a product of the giant dam at Boulder, hundreds of miles away. And you know that besides the dam at Boulder there are the dams of the Tennessee Valley Authority, the Grand Coulee Dam, the Shasta Dam and all the others. At once sublimely simple in their conception and infinitely complex in their detail, these dams are probably the only perfect and blameless instruments created by human beings in this villainous century.

We came to southern California to find the sun which would make Dorothy strong and better able to endure future winters in Canada and we have found it. This is a season of drought in southern California and we are sorry for everyone who longs for rain, but for us the weather has been wonderful—warm enough to go without coats or sweaters during the day, cool enough to sleep under blankets at night.

Having paid your respects to the weather, anything else you can think of saying about southern California is likely to be true. It is the home of Frank Sinatra and Thomas Mann, it is filled with top-ranking athletes and old men with bad hearts, it is the voting place of crack-pots and some of the most genuinely kind and simple people you can find anywhere. Aside from Hollywood, the towns are gracious, without the ugliness of the last century and the general vulgarity of the present one. Yet vulgarity of mind is not lacking in southern California, as anyone who gets around can tell you, though it shows up out here with even greater vividness in religious life than it does in the productions of Hollywood. An entire page of the *Los Angeles Times* is given over each Saturday to advertisements for divine service. Many of the churches promise motion pictures in place of a sermon. Last Sunday the minister of a church in Los Angeles advertised as his morning text, "Home-town Boy Makes Good" (the home town presumably being Nazareth). In the evening his text was, "Girls! Have You the New Look?"

Living out here for a space of time, one is conscious of the fact that California is inhabited by people from all over the United States and from half the countries of the world. In its point of view on world affairs, California is a suburb of New York. There is little jingoism here on the top layers of thought and there is much good nature. Politics in California are notably clean.

So our trip across the continent has ended on a bluff overlooking the ponderous, blue Pacific. While our days on the road gave me no positive information about the rôle of the United States in the future, they did convince me that the views of congressmen and senators as expressed in Washington reflect—if not a thorough distillation of the views and prejudices of the districts which elect them—a certain clue to the character of their constituents. This trip has also reinforced my conviction that the East is still the most important and hopeful area of the United States. More brains and experience, more germinating ideas and a sharper sense of the realities of our century can be found in the old, settled areas near the Atlantic than in the rest of the country put together. The time-lag which exists between the eastern cities and the hinterland is rendered even greater by the fact that the most brilliant men of the hinterland tend to move East to make their careers.

Americans are afraid today with an honourable fear, for on the whole they are more afraid of themselves than of any possible war. They are asking how their traditional democracy can survive in a world in which their power has become so great that each of their acts sends waves of repercussions around the world. They are bewildered and some of them are angry, because their domestic policy can no longer be separated from their foreign policy. They dislike the idea of an increasing self-restraint. Worst of all, their almost mystical belief in the wisdom of democratic voters is being shaken.

A world dominated by scientific experts is far too complicated for the ordinary voter to understand, no matter where he lives. Foreign affairs are complex and finely balanced. It follows, therefore, that American policy cannot be made by the people in the sense that it could once be made. While the people can, and should, curb the ambitions of politicians, there is little doubt that policy will more and more be created by small groups of brilliant men who control public opinion and the political machinery in Washington. And few of these men will be elected to office by the people.

In spite of the fact that this situation has always existed to some extent, it is resented in the United States more than it would be in Canada because it cuts directly across a myth in which Americans have been encouraged to believe from their childhood, namely, that the ordinary citizen, the Mr. Smith who goes to Washington devoid even of the qualifications required to govern a village, will be so fortified by the spirit of democracy that somehow or other he will stump the experts. As a result, a disproportionate number of politicians are tempted to pretend to being more stupid than they are, and politics and politicians have become more cynical than they would in an atmosphere where the voters frankly face the fact that while God may have created all men equal, he did not create all men with equal abilities.

Whether or not the United States can become the first world citizen instead of the first world power will depend, in my opinion, on the success of American leaders in pointing out the difference between ends and means, between civilization itself and the productive methods which feed and clothe it. Can America integrate the exhausted remnants of Christian civilization and set them on the road to a new advance under her spiritual and political leadership? At the moment, far too much thinking in Washington has committed itself to the assumption that peoples like the Greeks and the Italians will become better at politics if they are taught American methods of production.

Mass production has made the United States the most powerful country in history. It has made its citizens the wealthiest. But in feeding the body it has starved the spirit; by its very success it has persuaded millions of people, Socialists and Communists as well as capitalists, that the production, acquisition and distribution of material goods is the final purpose of human life.

As a result, Henry Ford is closer today than Thomas Jefferson to the lives of most Americans and though they talk with pride of their freedom, they tend to assume that their advanced status in civilization is due as much to their productive and business methods as to the great human vision of their Founding Fathers. When the National Association of Manufacturers speaks of "the American Way of Life," it is Ford's way it has in mind.

The logical human product of the worship of mass

production as an end in itself is Babbitt. The logical human product of the ideas of the Founding Fathers is Abraham Lincoln and Bill Mauldin. Jefferson and Franklin knew perfectly well that the ancient European culture was a priceless heritage, for they were a part of it. They knew that it reached its greatest height in the balance of science and art which was Leonardo da Vinci and its greatest loveliness in the refined fusion of thought and feeling still to be heard in the music of Mozart. Babbitt would neither know nor care that the price of mass production, of the puritan conception that what a man does can be separated from what a man is, has been the final extinction of the spirit which made the music of Mozart possible.

Because the future of the whole world, whether we live or die, depends to a large extent on what happens within the United States, the time has come when non-Americans—and Canadians in particular—must assume the right to speak candidly of conditions within the United States. I know that many Americans will consider this point of view a presumption. Yet the world would be both safer and happier if they would realize that when foreigners criticize Americans they are not implying the possession of more wisdom and virtue in themselves. They are merely asserting the obvious. They, too, have a vital interest in the future of America. They are assuming that the United States is the most important country in the world.

6

PORTRAIT OF A CITY

Sometimes it is almost as important for a man to know where he came from as to guess where he wants to go.

As I have already indicated in the foreword to An Orange from Portugal, *there are two kinds of truth for a writer: emotional truth and the verity of judgment based upon fact. I have discovered from experience that I cannot write with sound factual judgment of the town where I grew up. I see it always with the eyes of a child who came to know it at the age of seven without any predisposition to like it and knowing nothing whatever about it. Had my original emotions with relation to Halifax been unpleasant, I should now be inclined to distort my vision of it shamelessly to suit that dislike. But it happens that I admire Halifax and always have, from the day I first arrived from Cape Breton with my parents and stood on a corner watching one of those crazy little street cars bucking along Barrington Street. So I am prepared without apology to show my affection for it now.*

There have been times in my life when I have been unhappy; on at least two occasions I have been close to despair. But I have seldom been bored, and for this I owe Halifax a lot. No man can possibly be bored for long if his sensations of touch, smell, sight and sound have been as adequately stimulated in his youth as mine were by that old seaport.

PORTRAIT OF A CITY

A FEW years ago, while travelling in the West, I happened to mention to a train-companion that I considered Halifax one of the few authentically beautiful cities in Canada. He smiled, like a polite man showing the required appreciation of a feeble joke. Then, seeing that I was serious, he burst out: "My God, have you ever been there?"

"Have you?" I asked.

"I was stationed in Halifax for two hundred and forty-seven days and if——"

To set down the rest of what the man said would be redundant, for you have heard it all before. He repeated most of the usual charges levelled against Halifax by inland Canadians during the war—the fleecing of service men by lodging-house keepers, the liquor law, the drabness, the lack of amusements for seamen exhausted by weeks of convoy duty in the North Atlantic. It never occurred to him that the same charges would have held good against any other Canadian town of similar size, if any other Canadian town had been saddled with a similar wartime job. Least of all did he realize that the war had nothing important to do with the feeling of frustrated anger which Halifax has always occasioned in the majority of inland Canadians. Long before 1939 Halifax was uniquely unpopular, and the reason for this unpopularity is an interesting sidelight on our national character.

Canadians of the interior generally take one look at Halifax and conclude that by all rules of comparison familiar to them, their own cities are vastly superior. Being a sensitive people, who wince with anger and guilt when they themselves are censured, they begin by criticizing Halifax gently. Haligonians don't listen. The inland voices rise higher as it becomes more necessary that Haligonians should admit a self-evident inferiority and search out ways of self-improvement. Haligonians don't even pay them the compliment of getting angry. Finally, the horrible truth reveals itself. Not only do Haligonians not give the smallest damn what hinterlanders think about Halifax; they don't care what hinterlanders think about anything on earth.

No, Halifax is not unpopular on account of her rôle in the war. She is unpopular in exactly the same way that an incorrigible boy is unpopular with his school-teachers. But there is more than this moral insensitivity to be set in the scales against the city. There is also a wealth of factual detail.

If you like Winnipeg, with its well-lit streets open to the cleansing winds, how can you endure Halifax, where flickering arc lamps loom through the fog in streets as narrow as those of Dickensian London?

If you admire London (Ontario), a city so clean, progressive and business-like that Americans feel it would be a credit to Ohio, how can you admire Halifax, which for years has been dirty, reactionary and mockingly indifferent to the entire North American ideal of progress?

If you admit the superiority of Toronto, where serious drinking has been confined until recently to well-kept homes and hotel bedrooms, where love-making in private is modified by the discipline of the people and in public is impossible, what good word can you find for Halifax, where, in certain areas, bottles are tilted on street corners at high noon, and on warm evenings the park and the slopes of the Citadel are murmurous with sailors and the girls they have picked up on the lower streets?

Or perhaps you come from Montreal, our one city famous for tolerance. What then can you make of the attitude of the better families of Halifax, who are as strict as people in Ontario, and have been convinced for years that Halifax *as a whole* leads a sober, upright and godly life?

There is only one conclusion to be drawn from such a variety of pictures. Whether you love Halifax or not you must admit that she has character. She is distinct.

Whenever I hear Halifax condemned, I remember the great definition of Lord Bacon. "There is no excellent beauty that hath not some strangeness in the proportions." All the proportions of Halifax are strange. She sits there on her ironstone, generally in the wet, with all her faults exposed. Her face is towards Europe; her back (which is the city dump) greets strangers from the continent. The smells of tar, fish-meal, bilge, ozone, salt water, spruce forests and her own slums are rich in her nostrils. She is like an old trollop, lying in wait for weary seamen, if that is how you choose to regard her.

She is like an old lady living in genteel poverty amid the disorder of her own past, if you think of her more gently. But, because all her imperfections are inherent in her nature, inherent even in her function, Halifax comes close to satisfying Lord Bacon's definition. She possesses the same kind of beauty Rembrandt discovered in the battered faces of the old men and women he loved best to paint.

But these are generalizations. What I should like to do is to tell you why this city seems uniquely fascinating to me, who grew up there and still love her well.

There is no city in Canada, there is none in North America, which so amazingly concentrates life, in all its aspects, in a space so small. In most cities on our continent, the poor are separated from the well-to-do by railway tracks or by miles of streets. In the older parts of Halifax, the slums are back to back with the homes of the best families. You may dine in a house filled with antiques, rich in books, with old paintings on the walls. But a walk of a few minutes will take you to a boarding-house for seamen where you will encounter characters who could have walked out of a Conrad novel, and see rooms where, in living memory, drugs were put into the rum, and bos'ns and hard-case mates lurked in the back room with blackjacks in their pockets.

A boy growing up in Halifax may see life small, but he will see it as clearly as if he were watching through the large end of the telescope. It is so compressed and vivid that he can see, grasp, smell, feel and understand the whole interdependent organism.

When I was in fifth grade, the boy one seat ahead of me smelled constantly of dried sweat and fish. He was six years older than anyone else in the class because it had always taken him two and a half years to complete a single grade. At night he was too worn out from chores to do his home work, and frequently he disappeared for months at a time to go to sea. His hands were huge and horny, his fingers were permanently bent at the second joint from pulling on an oar since he had been old enough to sit upright on a thwart. He had a squint in one eye, his hair stuck out stiff over his forehead and he had lost his two upper front teeth. He was cheerful, friendly and gentle, and it never occurred to him to take advantage of his manifest superiority to the rest of us.

The boy opposite him spoke in what would sound to inland ears like an English accent. He wore the type of tweed britches, tight at the knees, then popular on golf links. His family lived in a fine house with gardens and walls about three sides of it, a pile of cannon balls by the front door and a small eighteenth-century muzzle loader pointing outward from the bottom step.

In front of this boy was a girl whose father was a lawyer, then a minister's son, then the daughter of a policeman. But alone at a corner desk was a boy who smelled so formidable that the teacher had been careful to seat him to leeward of the entire class. This boy had no father at all, and he was so tough and truculent that he ruled over us like a prince, receiving as his daily tribute the soggy apple cores of half the class.

Besides this concentration of life, which was a product of the city itself, the history of the era found in Halifax a vivid and sometimes terrible focus.

At least once a day, during that year, we would bolt from our seats to look out at the passing troops. The road was unpaved then, and the soldiers would trudge past on their route marches with the dust puffing up to their knees in the hot weather, and in winter with rime on their collars and the steam of their breath hanging over them like a cloud. We would watch them and wonder which ones would be killed. If they passed at recess-time, the boys would run along their flanks searching for familiar faces. "Look, there's Daddy! He's a captain!" And another boy might shout, "That's nothing, my father's a private!" There might easily be a fight over this.

One cold, clear December morning, while the boys were playing on the packed ashes about the school, and the first fight of the day was brewing, there was a roar past all hearing, and we saw the windows of the school burst inward and the trees toss, and a teacher stagger out the front door with blood streaming from her face. During the following hours as the sky darkened first with smoke, then with clouds, and finally with the snow of a driving blizzard, we saw the north end of the city in flames and the dead and wounded streaming south in slovens, ash and garbage carts, wagons, cars, baby carriages, trucks, ambulances, in anything that would roll.

Later each of us had his own stories of the great explosion. The father of one boy knew a man who was blown from the fo'c'sle head of a ship in the harbour to the slope of Fort Needham, three-quarters of a mile away; the man struck the ground on the exact angle of his flight, skidded to a stop and walked away naked. Another boy went home to find that his house had disappeared. Three days later his father found him and told him that his mother and five brothers and sisters were all dead. While the boy wept, his father comforted him by saying, "Never mind, I'll get you a new mother and start in all over again. Inside six years we'll have a family again."

The last year of the war saw the schools working in

double shifts.   So vivid was the sense of destiny in Halifax in those days that, even as schoolboys, we were aware of it.   To this day I can't watch water running down ice-rutted streets in the spring without feeling a recurrence of the mood of despair which struck Halifax on March 22, 1918, when the first reports of Ludendorff's great offensive reached home.   The snow was melting, a grey mist hung over us as it hung over the trenches in France, half of Halifax was in ruins, all of us had seen dead bodies, and now it seemed that the war was going to be lost.

But the war ended soon afterwards, the customary riot occurred in Halifax, and a year or two later our days in grammar school ended, too.   Some boys went to work, others of us passed on to the old Academy on the crest of Sackville Street.

Immediately the atmosphere in which we moved became subtly different.   In the lower grades life had seemed raw and exciting.   Now we became conscious that it is out of dangers that civilizations arise, and that we lived in a province with a great tradition of culture and adventure.   The embodiment of that tradition, as I knew it, was the senior master in the Academy, the finest teacher I have ever known.   No portrait I could draw of Halifax would be complete without him.   Even the setting in which he worked was appropriately symbolic.

His classroom was on the top floor of the Academy, with one set of windows facing east to the inner harbour, another set looking south to the open sea.   While we worked at set exercises, he used to stand in the window-bay with his fingers on a globe, his head domed like that of a Roman senator of the great period, his blue eyes looking out over the roofs to the lighthouse and the blink of the horizon.   Latin was the subject he nominally

103

taught, and we learned a lot of it from him. But what he really taught us was respect for life—not life as it might be, not life as it ought to be, but life as it is.

This man was sixty years old when I first saw him, and he had just left the army after four and a quarter years of war, more than two of which he had spent in the front line with a regiment which must have contained at least seventy of the boys he himself had once taught. In the summers he worked on a farm and read the classics by night. He must have known half the male population of Nova Scotia, he liked nearly all of them and the only things for which he never forgave his province were the attempts it made to copy the rest of the continent in standardizing education, as well as the asinine liquor law imposed by the shameless self-righteousness of a few dry counties. He was the only teacher I have ever met with no desire to change or reform people. Though he drove us hard, he relished enormously the more colourful characters among us, including one boy with a villainous face who chewed tobacco and later did well in the smuggling trade. He nourished two and a half generations of Haligonians, and even after his eightieth year, Halifax remained to him the same exciting, beautiful city it had been when he was a boy, when the docks were a forest of sailing ships and the streets were filled with men who had seen Joe Howe plain.

But Halifax, as we grew older, inevitably began to appear small. We wanted to turn the telescope around and look through the small end. We watched the ships sailing out over the horizon and some of us wished we were with them. As we neared the end of our high school days we realized that the city had subtly prepared us for the one solution Nova Scotia has discovered to balance her economic plight since the disappearance of wooden ships. Many of us knew we would have to emigrate whether we wanted to or not. Today at least half the boys I then knew well are scattered over the continent. Some are in England, one is even in Australia. We may still be parts of Halifax in our memories, but we are no longer Haligonians, and we know it.

The true Haligonians are the ones who were born in this outpost and have stayed behind to keep it up. Although the rest of Canada has not appreciated their efforts, there are many Canadian cities that could learn a lot from them. In spite of the fact that Halifax, before the Second World War, never had a permanent population in excess of seventy thousand, she has never acquired the atmosphere of a small town. The technique by which this catastrophe has been averted may be a deplorable one, but at least it has worked.

A small town has been defined as a community of indeterminate size, dominated by women. Small town men may speak their minds at their lodge meetings, but the words they utter there have small weight compared to those spoken in the sewing circles. A small town needs few laws to tame the instincts of the male animal. The tongues of the women do it instead.

In Halifax, no situation even vaguely resembling this definition has ever existed. Not only do the women have no control over the actual running of the city, they don't even control its manners and habits. Their ignorance of much that goes on in the self-confident male world surrounding them is regarded by their men as a salutary therapeutic for the social peace of mind. From the founding of the city as a naval and military colony, the men of Halifax have held together in a solid club against the great enemy of masculine equanimity—loose information about their habits, occupations, friends and amusements among the women they love. Elderly Halifax men have told me astonishing things about other elderly Halifax men. But they would no more dream of telling these same stories to their wives than they would consider informing their wives of the exact size of their personal incomes.

Of course there are defects in this male domination which even a man must recognize. It is responsible for the city's eternal look of distinguished shabbiness; men don't care for appearances as much as women do. And it is certainly the reason why the only entertainments for which Halifax has ever been famous seem barbarous to compatriots of the interior.

In Admiralty House or Government House, Halifax can stage a ball more stately than can be seen in any other Canadian city. Yet these are not the entertainments that her older men still mention with wistful eyes. In the old days there were banquets from which officers, immaculate in mess jackets, were seen crawling on their hands and knees up the slope of Sackville Street to the fort on the top of the Citadel.

They tell me that Halifax has changed, and perhaps she has. Most certainly I will be told that I have libelled her, and perhaps I have done that, too. As a matter of statistical fact, the majority of middle-class citizens in Halifax really do lead the sober life they profess to lead. People are beginning to paint their houses, the women dress much better than they once did, and perhaps they are now on the verge of coming into their own. Halifax is even willing to admit that she is Canadian. The day seems past when a customs inspector on the dock can speak the words I heard in 1930: "Nova Scotians in Aisle A, aliens and Canadians in Aisle B." Perhaps the R.C.N.V.R. sailors who tore the city apart on VE-Day have taught Halifax that she is a part of Canada in spite of Confederation.

On a fine evening last August, after an absence of many years, I walked through the south end from the gates of the park to the slope of the Citadel. The odour of lime trees was sweet along the sidewalks, the trees were stately, everyone I passed looked quiet, comely and respectable. Traffic was far heavier than I had remembered it, and on a corner near where I once lived stood a large, three-storey modern garage. But when I crossed Sackville Street I knew suddenly and irrevocably that the changes were superficial.

A man was reclining on the grass on the slope of the hill. He was wearing a rough cloth cap with a broken peak, his face was lined and pock-marked, he wore no collar or tie and his shirt was secured at the neck by a large gilt stud. As I passed him, he leered at me, grinned, leaned on his elbow to scratch his backside, then took from the pocket of a soiled jacket a flask-shaped bottle which he tilted to his mouth.

I reached the top of the Citadel and looked out over the roofs to the sea. The western horizon was rose and saffron as it always is at this hour of a fine summer evening. As the first faint evening mists rose, the harbour bells began to sound in the distance. Darkness increased, and the harsh angles of individual buildings faded out. The city revealed herself as a unit in all her noble contours, compact about the shield-like slope of the Citadel. I understood that she would care little for my opinion of her, but at that moment I knew she was still beautiful.

7

THE ELEPHANT ON PARADE

Here is my first attempt at reporting.   I covered the Republican Convention in June, 1948, on assignment for Maclean's, *commissioned to do what is termed a think-piece.   Because the Republican Convention of 1952 will be in all essential details exactly like the one I attended, the theme of this article is not necessarily dated.*

As you can see, I came away from the convention assuming that Thomas E. Dewey was going to be the next president of the United States, so my thinking was orthodox in that direction. What I misjudged was not Dewey so much as the wonderful refusal of the American people to have its collective mind made up for it by pollsters, public relations experts and columnists. There is some comfort to be derived by so-called foreigners, who try to gauge American public opinion, when they see how sadly it can be misread now and then even by American newspapermen.

Had I thought of it at the time I wrote this piece, I might have pointed out that in Dewey and Truman two diametrically opposite aspects of American life confronted each other.   Dewey symbolized management, efficiency and organization.   Truman symbolized the far older American attitude which trusts in the ability of a plain man to do the right thing at the right time without thinking too much of the probabilities in advance. Truman must have reminded a great many American voters of their own fathers.

To millions of people in the United States, Dewey represented such familiar items in American life as business machines and black limousines. No matter how often he played with somebody's pigs for publicity purposes, he always managed to look like an ad for modern office equipment. He was a boy from a small town who had gone to the big city and in the process had changed. Truman had gone to the big city, too, but no one could forget he had come from Missouri. People felt intuitively that he had roots.

There is much that is both true and untrue in this broad comparison of the two presidential candidates, but it is pleasant, and reassuring as well, to know that modern devices of thought-control such as opinion polls and highly paid columnists are less efficient than clever people had assumed them to be. It is good to know that the United States still prefers to put its trust in a country store rather than in a business machine.

THE ELEPHANT ON PARADE

N̲o̲ o̲n̲e̲ seems willing at this time to predict what kind of a president Thomas Dewey will make if he is elected by the United States in November. Great national leaders, especially within a democracy, are usually one of three different species of men. One kind, the most colourless, is the pure administrator. Another kind, always the most beloved, is a national replica of the father-image which resides within us all. The third kind, the most dangerous, is a symbol of youth in revolt.

In times of prosperity, when bank accounts bulge and people are confident of handling their own affairs, they prefer an administrator. Coolidge, who did nothing to lessen their self-esteem, is still considered to have been a good president by men whose affairs flourished in the 20's.

In times of trouble, people invariably turn to the father-image. Franklin Roosevelt, with his fireside chats

113

and wonderfully reassuring voice, was the father-image incarnate. Significantly, he was elected in the depths of the depression.

In times of despair, when the government has been too long in the hands of flabby men, people usually turn to youth in revolt. Invariably, such a leader is a man who believes in strong central authority, whether he calls it Fascism, Communism or something else with a label which has a sufficient history to give sanction to his power. So far we have seen no successful examples of this type of leader in federal politics in Canada or the United States.

To a certain extent all three of the leading candidates at the Republican Convention of 1948 fell by nature and disposition into one of these three categories. Taft was certainly the father type but, unfortunately for his ambitions at this or any other time, he seems to the public the kind of father who discovers the most excellent and logical reasons why a daughter should not marry the man of her choice. Stassen was a symbol of youth in revolt, but such a vague one, and perhaps such a sane one, that he had aligned himself with a conservative party in a prosperous year and so was bound to find himself running in a political vacuum.

At the present moment the individual American, for all his anxieties about America's relations with the outer world, feels prosperous and fairly self-confident at home. He does not so much want to love his president, or to feel that his president loves him, as he wants to know that he has a man in the White House who understands his job. Thomas E. Dewey, the able administrator who longs to take on the most difficult task in the world, has contrived to make himself appear, at least to his own party, the answer to that desire. From the beginning of

114

the convention no one else had a chance of winning the Republican nomination.

Despite the fact that they often verged on sheer comedy, the processes by which Dewey was nominated need not have been disheartening to an admirer of American democracy. Societies perish, we are told, because they become too fastidious to employ the vulgar means necessary to ensure their self-preservation. If this is true, there is no need to worry about the durability of the United States so long as its destiny rests with the kind of men who nominated the Republican candidate. The men who voted Dewey in represent a certain type of man extremely common in the political life of the United States. So far as I know, only one of the delegates died that week. The rest of the 3,000-odd officials, delegates and alternates looked as fresh at the end as they looked at the beginning. They seemed able to think without giving themselves time to think. They were insensitive to noise, heat, sweat and chills. Abuse failed to touch them. Above all, they enjoyed their work enormously and never tired of it. If they had been the kind of men who couldn't stand the pace of such a week in Philadelphia, they would have been some place else.

The general pattern of the American political convention was set nearly a hundred years ago, long enough to have created a venerable tradition on this continent. Since then the conventions have merely increased in scope without changing their essential nature. If they now seem noisier and more vulgar than they once did, that is because modern technology in the form of radio and television has played its usual part in amplifying bad taste and making it available to millions who might otherwise have been unaware of it. Americans regard

115

the kind of behaviour seen at these conventions as a fact, a particularly American fact, and this circumstance makes it in their eyes oddly unalterable. Foreigners, too, often forget that although the United States is the most revolutionary of all countries in its techniques and manners, it is the most conservative of all in its political customs. Much of the behaviour pattern which survives at conventions is a great deal more important than Americans themselves realize. It shows that, while the United States may have assumed the leadership of the western world, Americans themselves still have a longing for the simple folkways of their own past and for the time when they could act as irresponsible children when they felt like it, knowing it made no difference if they did.

The air in Philadelphia in the third week of June was as humid as air can be without congealing into actual liquid. The air-conditioning apparatus in Convention Hall either did not work or did not exist, but the klieg lights necessary for telecasting worked only too well. Sometimes the temperature in the hall was over a hundred degrees

It was a killing, stupefying heat, yet for five days and nights the delegates and their alternates, the committee-men, the bosses, special pleaders, whoopers-up and ward heelers, together with thousands of men and women who had assembled from all over the nation to support their favourite candidate, kept up a pace which was at once majestically slow in the consummation of the vital business in hand and hectically frantic in all the details and methods surrounding it. In the humid air they were simultaneously boiled and dazzled by the klieg lights, which made them look unnatural to everyone, including the bar-flies who watched the proceedings by television in the comfort of their neighbourhood saloons. They snatched meals and drinks in crowded restaurants and bars. They attended morning sessions in the hall from eleven until two-thirty in the afternoon, and evening sessions from nine until long past midnight. On the night of the nominations it was five in the morning before the hall was finally cleared.

But Convention Hall was only one scene of their activities. The suites in the downtown hotels were kept open twenty-four hours out of twenty-four, and long past midnight the lobbies were still milling with throngs. The politicians chivvied the delegates like cheerful stoats. I never once saw a politician shake hands in a normal manner; he always used both hands, one grasping the stranger's right, the other his elbow or shoulder, while a look appeared in his eyes which said more eloquently than words that this was the first occasion when the stranger's real merit had been recognized and appreciated.

Throughout Philadelphia that week the noise was constant. When delegates staggered into their rooms for a few hours of rest they sometimes found strangers asleep on their beds. All week their ears were hammered by bands playing campaign songs, by the roar of traffic in crowded streets and by the overmastering roar of the orators, most of whom had learned their trade before the day of the microphone. Now their gravel voices were distorted and magnified a hundred times by the technical apparatus into which they bellowed the most furious oratory I have ever heard.

Joe Martin, normally the Speaker of the House of Representatives and for this week permanent chairman (there were three chairmen in all, not because one was likely to crack under the strain but because the honour must be shared), pounded a five-pound gavel on a two-inch board of solid oak. On the fourth day he fractured the oak, but he merely grinned as though he had given a public demonstration of the weakness of material objects in comparison with the toughness of a good man.

In fact everybody, with the possible exception of Senator Taft of Ohio and Governor Duff of Pennsylvania, was marvellously cheerful and good-natured. The politicians and crowds at Philadelphia, with their posters, icons, slogans, oratory, skull-duggery, deals, fixes, promises and abuse of their opponents, formed, when all aspects are considered, probably the most thoroughly good-natured assemblage one could convene in the world today.

And yet the convention was self-consciously serious in purpose and even in its more important aspects. Everyone who was there and everyone who thought about it knew that it might well turn out to be the most important political convention held in the United States since the one which nominated Abraham Lincoln on the eve of the Civil War. It was accepted as axiomatic at the convention that Harry Truman could not possibly be re-elected unless the Republicans made fools of themselves in their choice of a candidate or in their campaign during the following months.

There were times, as I sat in the section of the first balcony reserved for the periodical press, when I was overcome by a feeling of awe at the power of choice residing with the 1,094 delegates below me. The presidency is such a tremendous position, far greater and more isolated than that of Prime Minister. Good or bad, weak or strong, the President is elected for a minimum of four years and nothing short of impeachment can oust him during that time. There the delegates sat, row by row under their state placards, their alternates grouped in similar fashion behind them, two for every senator and representative sent by their respective states to the Congress, with a few more delegates as bonuses to those states which had voted Republican in 1944 or 1946.

They were a mixed group, containing both important and obscure men and women. At the head of the Pennsylvania delegation was the rugged figure of Governor Duff, a man of presidential capacity himself. In the Massachusetts section one could see the lean, shy, aristocratic features of Senator Saltonstall. There were several Negroes among the delegates. Glenn Cunningham, the famous middle-distance runner, sat in the Nebraska section. Irene Dunne and George Murphy of Hollywood were among the fifty-three from California. One delegate I met—and a quiet, thoughtful man he was—told me he was a veterinary from Indiana. Among these 1,094 there were certainly many, possibly a majority, who were only nominally of an independent mind. In some states it is the law that they must vote as a unit and in others they voted as their delegation chairman instructed. It was also a fact that a large number of them were motivated chiefly by a personal interest in showing themselves on the side of the winner.

There were a good many official and unofficial foreign observers at this Republican Convention in Philadelphia, and I suppose all of us were in some degree astounded by the realization that such a solemn act as the selection of the probable next President of the United States should be preceded by days of ward-heeling oratory and accompanied by outbursts of infantile frenzy of a kind indigenous only to this one country in all the world.

Yet it was in the pattern and each of us had to find a way to understand what we observed, remembering that hokum is an integral and time-honoured part of all conventions in the United States, whether those convening are shoe salesmen, sociologists, florists or politicians. It was soon evident that such a convention as this had two quite different and opposing reasons for being called. One of these was to provide a jamboree on a gigantic scale for the faithful. The other was the hardest kind of business. Inevitably, the business went on behind closed doors in the Bellevue-Stratford and the Benjamin Franklin hotels, while the jamboree was visible and audible not only in Convention Hall, but on millions of television and radio sets around the world.

On the first day it took the chairman more than half an hour to call the delegates to order. Then a girl with naked shoulders, a skin-tight aquamarine dress and a silver cummerbund around her waist, sang the national anthem. She was followed by the Methodist Bishop of Philadelphia, who in the invocation earnestly reminded the Republicans that they were sinners as he implored the Divine Being to quicken their shame at past wickednesses. It was a prayer that fell on stony ground, for the only wickednesses mentioned in that hall during the rest of the week were those of Democrats and Communists.

When the Bishop retired, he was followed by the Mayor of Philadelphia, the manner of whose introduction set the tone of all introductions to follow. "A man of the pee-pul," the chairman shouted, "beloved by the pee-pul!"

The Mayor was followed by entertainers, introduced as the best barbershop quartet in America.

A long speech by Governor Duff followed and it might have been interesting if the speaker himself had been interested in what he was saying. But, as we already knew, Governor Duff regarded his speech as a mere formality. The job he had set himself at the convention was to fight the Grundy-Owlet machine in his own key state and until Wednesday night that battle was not fought in public.

Following the Governor came Carroll Reece, the chairman of the National Republican Committee. This tireless man, who had spent days and nights helping to organize the convention, was in sight throughout its duration. Like all the orators, he had a mighty voice. Like all of them, he linked the New Deal and the Democratic administration with Communism, associated Franklin Roosevelt with the fact that America had been forced to participate in the war and afterward had lost the peace. The details of his address I forget, as I suppose he himself has forgotten them. But his peroration I shall remember whenever I see a politician grip a lectern with both hands and throw back his head to give me the business. "The American People," he bellowed, "do not belong to the Government. The Government belongs to the American People. And the American People"—he paused for several seconds, then let his voice drop to a microphone whisper—"belong only unto God!"

Through the next three days and nights there were many, many more speeches. After each one, the delegates from the orator's home state waved their state banner and as often as not got up to parade around the floor. The keynoter was the silver-haired, red-faced, tight-lipped Governor of Illinois, Dwight Green. In his address he employed the phrase "the American People" so often that I became hyponotized by it and lost all idea of what his speech was about. I well remember a Mrs. Frances Bolton of Ohio who, the chairman told us, "speaks as a mother." She did indeed. "We who know the cost of giving life," she cried passionately, "as NO MAN ever can or ever will—know that we cannot sit back at this grave moment in world history. Let me tell you that the WOMEN of America care! At election time in November they will show that they care!"

Mrs. Bolton was followed by the Coatesville Male Choir, which received from the chairman a truly Republican introduction. "This choir," he said, "contains insurance brokers, a schoolteacher, realtors and a banker—in short, a truly representative group from their community!" Their first offering was "The Wood-chuck Song."

So the sessions went on while the real work was being carried out in the hotels. Resolutions were offered and passed, an on-the-record platform was presented by Henry Cabot Lodge, Jr., and adopted.

An event of deep significance to Republicans occurred the night ex-President Herbert Hoover appeared to address them. The old man was as straight in the back and as stiff in the neck as ever, his hair very white, his face very pink. He received a tremendous ovation which may have atoned for some of the bitterness which has eaten into him over the past eighteen years.

Hoover was followed on the platform by Clare Booth Luce, who gave an address in which she ridiculed President Truman so mercilessly that even Westbrook Pegler objected to it the next day in his column. The quickness of Americans to sympathize with the underdog was never more clearly shown than by the reception of this speech. It was the kind which should have been made by nobody on any platform, least of all by a talented and beautiful woman. Her choice of metaphors would have been vulgar had they come from a man; coming from that exquisite woman they were shocking and they made many of the men in the audience extremely uncomfortable. "After all," one of the ushers said to me the next day, "maybe the guy hasn't got much on the ball, but he's a gentleman and he can't handle that dame the way she handled him."

There was another feature of the convention which, to my knowledge, none of the reporters troubled to mention, but which moved me, the outsider, more deeply than I have words to describe. Again and again the band played "The Battle Hymn of the Republic" and at least four times it was sung by stars from the operatic or concert stage. The Republican Party was and still is the political instrument of puritan America. It is puritan America with all its self-satisfied materialism; but deep down it is also puritan America in its flaming faith in the inviolability of the individual man. It was out of the spirit which won the Civil War, which the puritans waged to implement that faith, that the "Battle Hymn of the Republic" came, just as it was in the course of that war that the Republican Party established itself.

It was Wednesday before the names of the candidates were put in nomination and no one who was present in the hall that day is likely to forget it. It was during the course of the day that it became known that Senator Martin of Pennsylvania had bolted into the Dewey camp. It was at seven in the evening, in a small room boiling under klieg lights, that Governor Duff, too late to frustrate the Grundy-Owlet gang who were believed to have engineered Martin's desertion, threw the Pennsylvania caucus open to the public and had each member polled in the presence of witnesses. It was at nine in the evening that the session was convened for the nominations and by ten o'clock the temperature within the hall, inflamed by the body heat of more than two thousand frenzied delegates and alternates, rose to over a hundred degrees.

Neither radio nor television gave a fraction of the sense of pandemonium and organized chaos which broke out on that night. Each candidate was nominated in a fifteen-minute eulogy by his chosen henchman and the nomination speech was followed by four seconders who were allowed five minutes each. This called for a schedule of 270 minutes of oratory. At the end of each nomination there was a period of half an hour or more of insane yelling, parading, noisemaking and hoopla that is known technically as a demonstration.

Nearly all the nomination speeches ridiculed themselves. Senator Bricker, an imposing figure in size and stateliness, was so moved by his own words in praise of Senator Taft that for several moments it seemed doubtful if he would be able to finish. "No man," the reporter next to me murmured, "can possibly think so highly of anyone else. Bricker's going to end up by nominating himself." We watched him as his mighty voice rallied after a weak spell and he tossed his mane of silver hair and lunged back at the microphone. At the end he gave us the name—Robert Alphonso Taft! Then, his face as red as an explosion, he staggered back into the arms of Carroll Reece and Walter Hallanan, who pounded him on the back while he shook his head slowly from side to side, as if the majesty of his own oration had knocked him out.

The Taft demonstration was louder than Dewey's and milder than Stassen's, but it can stand as a sample of nearly all the rest. Before the final seconder had fallen silent, the Taft men took to the floor. It was nearly midnight then. Shirts were clinging to wet skins. Men sat with their jackets folded on their knees. There were still four and a half hours and five nominations to go.

Senator Taft's face does not look its best on an election poster and his henchmen had two pictures of him on each poster they carried, one side smiling, the other side grim. Under the ghastly glare of the klieg lights, the posters constantly rotating, constantly bobbing up and down, the face stern on one side, smiling on the other, stern and smiling faces dancing on hundreds of posters on the ends of poles until the whole floor looked like a forest of decapitated heads bobbing and dancing, the henchmen of Senator Taft went into a war dance that lasted nearly forty minutes. Why anyone should be moved to elect a man to a grave office after such a display no non-American will ever understand.

On that night Governor Warren showed the tact which marked his behaviour all through the convention. When his name was put into nomination by the California delegation, he allowed the demonstration in his honour to last ten minutes, then he requested his followers to leave the floor. Such modesty was not for Stassen's crowd. At three o'clock in the morning they were still under way, led by a drum majorette who mounted the rostrum to do a rumba while a girl in a boat was carried around the floor on the shoulders of the crowd. At four-something in the morning the nominations were finally over and the last one was probably the most instructive of them all.

Wisconsin, toward the end of the alphabetical list of states, had been unable to persuade Alabama or Arkansas to cede their right to nominate a favourite son in Wisconsin's favour. So Wisconsin waited her turn. A lonely soldier, who had spent most of the war years in a

Japanese prison, read a speech in praise of a military hero, his commanding officer. When he finished, the nomination was duly seconded, but there were no swaggering military bands as there would have been in Europe, no hokum as there had been earlier in the evening, no impressive swashbuckling to make up a demonstration. General MacArthur's name was recorded by a tired secretary on the platform and what was left of the crowds went home to bed. In seven hours the delegates were due back again to cast their votes.

To no one's surprise, probably not even to Senator Bricker's, Dewey won the nomination on the following day. He won it mainly by reason of his pre-convention organization, partly because of the hard and very clever work which had been going on in hotel rooms while we watched the jamboree in Convention Hall, partly also owing to the imponderables which always exercise an influence in affairs of this kind.

Dewey is a symbol of the force of management. As Governor of New York, by far the most complex of all the states, he has shown a good record, even though he inherited an excellent state of affairs from his predecessors, Governors Lehmann and Franklin D. Roosevelt. Dewey has surrounded himself with able men, managers like himself, who have done their best for him. As a man, he has a reputation for coldness, for a hard head and a calculating ambition. He is in general more respected than liked. In spite of his comparative youth, the radicals who follow Wallace hate Dewey worse than they hate Taft, probably because they regard him as a more formidable enemy.

Dewey's headquarters were quieter than Taft's and much quieter than Stassen's. The people who thronged his rooms in the Bellevue-Stratford were generally less

126

attractive people than those who so audibly adored Stassen. But nearly all of Dewey's followers had the air of men and women who are accustomed to getting what they want, who will get it nine times out of ten.

When Dewey held his first press conference, he sat on a chair under klieg lights and answered questions for over half an hour. His hands were folded on the table before him, his voice was quietly modulated, his answers were quick, good-humoured and to the point and every one of them worked to his advantage. During this half-hour of questioning Dewey appeared to be completely reposed. He never moved a muscle below those of his neck; his legs, arms and small body remained still and relaxed. Such control and self-confidence were almost disconcerting in a man who looked so young, for in spite of the responsibilities he has held in his life, Dewey could pass for a man under forty. No photograph does him justice, because no photograph reveals the nature of his eyes. In pictures, the height of Dewey's frontal bones and cheekbones obscures the eyes with shadows and makes them look opaque. In life they are very large, luminous and dark, and he has a way of rolling them occasionally, whether to express irony or amusement I could not tell. He disparaged no antagonist in his interview; instead he contrived to give everyone the feeling that the sooner the convention was over the better, since the result was so clearly a foregone conclusion.

When the convention was over, it was all too apparent that Harold Stassen had represented no real force at all. He had merely stood for a point of view, a point of view shared by millions of well-meaning Americans who desire no radical change but who would like to see a younger man, free of the taint of party bosses, at the head of the Government. Were 1948 a depression year, I have little doubt that Stassen would have won the nomination, for I got the distinct impression that, whereas Dewey would be more at ease dealing with individuals, Stassen would be happiest dealing with a crowd.

One is forced to believe that a large portion of the relief felt in the United States over Dewey's winning of the nomination is based on a deep thankfulness that the Republican nominee is not Robert Taft, for in American life today he represents the bitter reaction of pure isolationism. In him is lodged all the Middle Westerner's naïve conviction that nothing but harm can come from Europe, that things were better forty years ago than they are now because forty years ago labour was less obstreperous, that the United States will prosper if she stands aloof and will come to harm if she associates freely with the corruption of Europe and Asia. There are still many voters in the United States who hold Taft to be completely right in such judgments. Around him the Republican Old Guard of the Harding-Coolidge-Hoover era stood firm. This should be a Republican year according to the bosses, but fortunately they could feel the will of the people even in the small hours of the morning in the closed suites of the hotels. "Dewey," an American reporter said to me, "is the least liberal candidate they thought they could get away with."

On the night the third ballot was completed and Dewey was nominated by acclamation there was a long period during which we waited for him to reach Convention Hall in order to deliver his acceptance speech. Now we could see a small brigade of police officers formed in a double line, marking the path Dewey would have to take to the rostrum. Within a matter of seconds, the very instant after he had been officially acclaimed the nominee, he had become a public charge. Dewey was now a precious cargo, he was a ward of the state and he was guarded carefully even from the very crowd which had given him that honour.

When he finally appeared, intense, petite, his face was radiant with happiness. He opened his arms wide to receive the emotion of the crowd while Mrs. Dewey stood aside, her own dignity grave and retiring. And because it was a North American crowd, reared fundamentally in the British tradition of politics, even though it contained hundreds of bitter opponents of Dewey, it gave him a warm and earnest ovation as it responded generously to his simple speech of humility and promise.

Now he faces the entire country. Whether he can beat Harry Truman in November depends neither upon his promises nor his trained radio voice, but solely upon the effect of Russian strategy on the unconscious needs of the American people through the summer and fall of 1948.

8

"HELP THOU MINE UNBELIEF"

No piece of non-fiction I ever wrote brought in such a flood of mail, not to mention telephone calls, as did this article when it first appeared in print. Some of the letters, especially the ones from clergymen of many faiths, I was more than glad to have. But taken as a drawerful, those mostly over-long letters were disconcerting. They showed me that in a discussion of religious matters today it is impossible to proceed on the assumption that ordinary English words will be taken to mean exactly what they say. Nearly all my correspondents had widely diverging religious views, yet with one single exception they all seemed to think that my article was a corroboration of their personal opinions.

The title which the piece bears in this volume is the one I suggested when it was delivered to the magazine for publication. I still shudder to think what the result might have been had the editor used it. The title which he chose in its place—Are We a Godless People?—brought a fountain of unsolicited advice. What would an implied plea for assistance have produced, quotation marks or not?

"HELP THOU MINE UNBELIEF"

A FEW years ago, while I was still teaching in a boys' school in Montreal, I had occasion to mention during one of my classes that the oldest writings in the New Testament were the Epistles of St. Paul, and that the oldest gospel was that of St. Mark.

When the class was over, one of the boys waited behind to speak to me. He was seventeen, a good student (especially in the sciences), gentlemanly, good-natured, imaginative and courageous. He was the son of one of the most eminent medical men in the city.

"Excuse me, sir," he said, "something you said today reminded me of a question I've been wanting to ask for some time, only I forgot. Those men Paul and Mark you were talking about—who were they?"

From the expression on his face I knew he was not being flippant, nor was I as astounded then as I am now when I recollect this incident. When one works with a

133

generation which draws most of its cultural food from comic strips and the radio, one finds one's self prepared for almost anything. I asked him if he had ever heard of the Bible.

"It's a book, isn't it?"

"Haven't you ever been to church?"

"My father says only ignorant people and Roman Catholics go to church."

"Did your father ever go to church himself?"

"He did when he was a boy, but he didn't like it."

"How old is your father?"

"Forty-seven or forty-eight."

I explained to him briefly who Paul and Mark were, and let the matter drop. A few days later he came to me in a state of some bewilderment.

"Sir," he said, "you were talking about the Bible the other day. Well, I've been reading it. Why is that book famous?"

"Why do you think it shouldn't be?"

"But those people were very ignorant."

"Who were ignorant?"

"Most of the people in the book." He looked at me as though an idea had struck him. "Did all that happen?"

"How much of the Bible did you read?" I asked.

"I read some of the new part. I mean, was this man Jesus killed like that or is it just a story?"

"He was really killed like that."

"Was He God's son any more than I am?"

"He told His disciples He was."

He was silent and seemed to be thinking hard. "It keeps saying you've got to believe that or you'll be ruined. That isn't true. My father doesn't believe it and he's done very well."

134

I had nothing to say to this.

"It keeps on talking about faith," the boy went on. "I looked that word up in the dictionary and it says faith means having complete confidence in someone or something open to question or suspicion. I don't see anything good about that."

"Why not?"

"Science teaches you never to believe anything unless you can prove it." Then he looked puzzled and said, "I don't understand why people took all that stuff seriously. God just wasn't very intelligent."

Looking at the earnest face, I knew that the boy was sincere. Even at seventeen, he had retained the poignant eagerness to do the right thing which is one of the loveliest characteristics of a nice child.

"Perhaps," he conceded, "it was a good idea at that time in history."

"What was a good idea?"

"This business of sending Christ to show people how to live."

"You mean, it was a good idea two thousand years ago in the sense that the Wright brothers' airplane was a good machine for 1903?"

He brightened somewhat, but he did not yield. "No, sir, not exactly. After all, modern aircraft have been developed from the original idea of the Wright brothers, but it's two thousand years since Jesus lived and the history master told us that people are just about the same now as they were then."

I have recorded this dialogue, not with the intention of being shocking or flippant, but because to me it illustrates more clearly than any amount of argument how abrupt has been the fracture with two thousand years of religious tradition. I was nearly twenty years older than this pupil of mine, and twenty years is a very short period when measured in terms of world history. Yet I believe it would have been impossible for a similar case to have existed when I was at school. Even if the boy had been brought up in a family of militant atheists, he could hardly have talked like this. He would at least have been aware of the identity of St. Paul and St. Mark. He would have lived and moved, whenever he left his home, in an atmosphere in which people were conscious of religion. Yet this boy had gone for eight years to a school where every morning he had listened to a brief prayer read to the assembled boys from the Prayer Book. If he had ever thought of this ritual at all, he had apparently decided that it was intended as a technique to make the whole school fall quiet for half a minute in the locker-rooms before marching up to their classes to begin the day's work.

As I walked home that night, I turned over in my mind what seemed to me the salient points raised by my discussion with this boy. His father was a middle-aged man of scientific training who had apparently carried the logic of his thinking into his active life and that of his family. Beyond this, how different was he really from the majority of city-dwelling Protestants of his own age, training and education, who go to church for the music on Easter, eat turkey and sing carols at Christmas, and feel that the Christian religion, while it bores them, is probably a good thing for other people and certainly can be relied upon to provide ringing slogans during a war?

The second point that seemed to me significant was the boy's unquestioning acceptance of the scientific attitude. If a point of view appeared to conflict with what his untutored mind assumed to be scientific procedure, he was prepared to believe immediately that such a point of

136

view was wrong. Here, surely, was a new form of bigotry which the scientists themselves encourage.

Finally, there was the North American attitude which regards everything as a "project." He had even reduced Christ's mission to the world as a project, and had decided that time had proved it to be outmoded.

With this analysis I dropped the matter for the time being. But for months, and then for years, I kept remembering this discussion whenever I heard people examining the plight of religion today. Again and again I read, as you also have read, that the spirit of the Christian religion is dying, and that compared to the world of our grandfathers, Protestant North America has largely become a pagan civilization.

That orthodox religion in the Protestant churches, at least as our forefathers understood it, has suffered a profound decline is a fact which nobody denies today.

We have been told recently that the enrollment in the churches of North America has shown considerable increase since the beginning of World War II, but I believe there are few clergymen who take much comfort from these figures.

How many of those affiliated with the Protestant churches attend service regularly? How many of the highly educated group who are members of what Professor A. J. Toynbee calls "the creative minority" go to church at all unless they are Roman Catholics?

When Canadians compare themselves to the citizens of other lands, they probably have some reason to claim that they are living in a religious country. Certainly no part of the Roman Catholic world is more deeply devout than French-speaking Canada, and the Protestant churches still represent a considerable force. Yet among Protestants of advanced education, especially among college graduates, the same phenomenon is occurring in Canada now as occurred in the United States a generation earlier. They are leaving the churches. So are the young people. This is true even in small towns.

Canada, one might say, has the habit and perhaps the desire for religion; she is by no means exultant in her growing drift away from it, but it would be a travesty on the meaning of the word to claim that Protestant Canada is still a religious community.

In recent years I have made enquiries among many of my friends on this subject. Most of them are professional men: doctors, lawyers, newspapermen, writers, scientists, professors, research workers, men in public life. Their unvarying response is a curious one. Hardly one is prepared to call himself an atheist, yet hardly one of them goes to church as often as once a year. Many tell me they discover their greatest religious release in art and music. Some say they have no religious interests at all. None of them—and I mean absolutely none with the exception of one or two who are actually clergymen—find any satisfaction whatever in the services of an established church, though one man admitted that he occasionally goes to a service because it reminds him of his childhood.

I have frequently been asked by worried parents whether I think they should send their children to Sunday school even though they don't themselves believe what their children will be taught. This question has always seemed to me singularly pathetic. It amounts to saying, "When I was young I believed in fairy tales and I was happy. Now I am lonely, and though I'm too old to believe any longer I'd like my children to have the same advantages I was once given."

Another complaint we constantly hear is directed against the clergy. We are told again and again that the churches are not meeting modern needs. In my opinion, any non-Catholic who seriously blames the clergy for the decline of the churches is merely looking for a scapegoat. The Protestant churches are not sacerdotal; they are democratic assemblies. They are neither better nor worse than the people who compose their congregations. To blame those ministers who made fools of themselves in the United States at the time of the so-called monkey trial at Dayton is justifiable. To blame fanatics who stir up agitations for prohibition in the name of the Christ who turned water into wine is the part of a good citizen. To feel indignation at self-righteous puritans who would make little children feel guilty for their human nature, while at the same time withholding from them the release of confession and absolution, is natural and right. But to blame the Protestant clergy as a whole for the present state of the Protestant faith is a gross injustice to men who are virtually forbidden by their own congregations to raise any issues which would make those congregations uncomfortable.

It would be far more sensible to blame nobody—to forget this futile, haunting, primitive sense of guilt which is the worst legacy of puritanism—while we try in all humility to understand what is happening to our spiritual lives.

Religion can never be anything save a thing of the spirit: its values are of the spirit, its aims are of the spirit. But the society in which we live has become so increasingly materialistic that even our standards of goodness are generally materialistic ones. It is not a change in our judgment of what constitutes evil that marks the

139

extent of our drift from our spiritual past. It is the change in our judgment of what is good.

In the past, a man's goodness was primarily measured by his devotion to God, by his service to God, and neither of these phrases then seemed mysterious or obscure. Today a man's goodness is measured—at least in the non-Catholic world—by his material services to his fellow man.

A Protestant today who lived a life of poverty in order to meditate on the divine would be considered to have lived a worthless life, and might even be advised to consult a psychoanalyst. On the other hand, a man who never gave a thought to the things of the spirit, but who organized boys' camps, or promoted slum clearance, or led a political crusade to clean the graft out of civic government—this man, if he was also kind to his family, would be considered an ideal human being.

Today, more than ever before, a man's goodness is judged by his work, by his co-operative attitude toward society as a whole. Here, in the ultimate test of human worth, is revealed our true sense of values. Man, not God, is the master who must be served. The present human world, not the divine eternal world, is the one which counts.

This state of affairs signifies one thing very clearly. Our Protestant society may be a good society in the human sense of the word good, but it has completely lost sight of its old religious goal. It can perhaps be called a Christian society still, but it can no longer be called a religious one. Therefore it stands in great danger.

History reveals clearly that no civilization has long survived after that civilization has lost its religion. Our own recollections of happenings in the present century should show us a danger which is far more imminent than the prospects of a slow decline, for where religion is concerned nature abhors a vacuum.

Nationalism, Fascism and Communism, as everybody should know by this time, are fundamentally neither political nor economic movements. They are, in their appeal to the masses and even to intellectuals, aberrations of the religious impulse. They are religious in their appeal because they provide materialistic-minded people with an easily recognizable master whom they can serve, an easily recognizable purpose which seems to make sense out of the mystery of human existence. They are aberrations because their dogmas are founded on hatred rather than on love, and it is this quality of hatred which makes them hideous creations, so destructive and dangerous that they will bring about the extermination of the human race unless their growth is arrested. But their growth cannot be checked by material force alone. It will shrivel only when confronted with a countervailing idea.

Does Christianity contain a countervailing idea great enough and sustaining enough to save society from totalitarianism and our own souls from the materialistic desert in which they now wander?

As Christianity is at present taught and understood, we delude ourselves if we think it can save us. It is at least a century since a new vision of the Christian "idea" has excited a multitude anywhere in the world.

The churches were helpless to prevent two appalling wars, they have surrendered their principles again and again to various national states, and only in the last two years, aided by the Marshall Plan, has the Roman Catholic Church been strong enough to arrest the growth of totalitarianism in even one country.

141

A character in one of my novels, an airman writing from a base in England while waiting for the bombers to return from a night raid, puts down these lines in a letter: "I seem to be haunted by the fact that at a time when more of us have good will in our hearts than ever before, the organized doing of evil has become our chief industry." This same comment, phrased somewhat differently, was made to me by a young airman during the war. It seemed to me then, and it still does, to contain the essence of our modern spiritual agony. As individuals we lead on the whole kindly lives. But as nations we are proud, cruel, wanton, vindictive and more often than not destructive.

Individual decency stems largely from our acceptance of much of Christ's ethics in our daily lives. National wickedness derives from our loss—in some cases total—of the idea of a divine providence.

Mankind, having lost his nearness to the traditional God of the Christian religion, having come more and more to think of Christ as merely the most perfect human being who ever lived, has for over a century been striving frantically to recreate the God idea he has lost in the shape of a national state. It is our tragedy that this effort has been largely successful.

A great national state, no matter what its pretensions, rests fundamentally on power and on nothing else. At best it stands for the order of the policeman, as Rome, Britain and the United States have stood or now stand for order. At worst it is an instrument of brutal aggression. But it can never stand for love.

Nationalism takes infinitely more than it can ever give. In the name of the state the most monstrous crimes are not only justified, they are demanded. Merciful Americans, who would have been horrified if they saw their neighbour kick a dog, rejoiced when they heard on their radios that the atomic bomb had been dropped on Hiroshima.

If the state of mind resulting from our loss of the sense of God's nearness constitutes the greatest crisis of our time, it surely behooves us at least to try to understand why this loss has occurred. It is my belief that it has occurred mainly because the symbols employed by the churches in explaining God to the people no longer seem valid in an age dominated by science.

God is at once purpose and cause. He is the cause of our existence and the purpose behind the universe. In Plato's language, God is the "self-moved mover of motion." In the language of the Christian church, God is an "infinite" being.

Because the human mind is unable to imagine infinity, it was the problem of the Christian theology to make an infinite God appear near and real to finite mortals. To do this, the church used symbols. Following the example of Jesus himself, the church constantly spoke of God in poetical and metaphorical language. "God is a spirit, and they that worship Him must worship Him in spirit and in truth." God, Jesus told us, is our heavenly father. Speaking of the hereafter, Jesus said, "In my Father's house are many mansions." Speaking of death it was said, "God will wipe away all tears and there will be no more death." The essence of Christian religion was that God would justify our existence if we justified ourselves to Him, and this we could do if we believed in Him, through the intercession of Jesus Christ and His redemption of man on the cross.

Until very recently this symbolic interpretation of purpose, of cause and of the infinite satisfied the bulk of people in the western world. Indeed, one has only to utter such phrases as these; to think such thoughts expressed in the old language; one has only to regard the serene beauty of medieval religious paintings; one need only listen to the sublimely humble confidence emerging from Bach's prelude called "Jesu, Joy of Man's Desiring" —to realize what a peace, what a glory and hope have passed away from the world with the loss of the idea of God's nearness.

"Man's chief end is to glorify God and enjoy Him forever." Who believes this today? Or, if he does believe it, is able to say so with the same simple confidence that he says the sun will rise tomorrow?

From the time when Copernicus upset medieval theology by proving that the earth was not the centre of the universe, science is said to have struck steadily at the heart of Christianity. It was science that weakened belief in the miracles as evidence of Christ's divinity and special mission. It was Darwin's theory of evolution which destroyed the validity of the Old Testament account of man's origin and original sin. Then Freud and the psychoanalysts, by their discovery of the workings of the subconscious, shattered the idea of God as a heavenly father by equating it with the subconscious yearning in all of us for the safety of our own childhood, when our earthly fathers stood between us and the blows of the world.

Above all else, science gave to the bulk of men in the West, especially to those who live in towns and cities, a new frame of reference. By causing men to live in proximity to machines, it made men think of causation as a mechanical process. It is no accident that farmers, close to the mysteries of germination, growth and death in the plant and animal world, are as a group more religious today than industrial workers.

All these things science has undoubtedly done. Yet what harm, in truth, has science done to essential religion save to create the surface illusion that it is less important than it was, to flatter us into believing we can become omnipotent, and to destroy the validity of the traditional symbols by which the church has tried to explain the idea of infinite God to finite man?

If the churches are taking stock of their position today, here surely is the essential point they should consider, and having considered it, take heart. Symbols are not now, and never have been, a reality. If the old ones stand between modern man and the reality of God, then new symbols must somehow be forged. For science has not even touched the cardinal idea of God.

Science, like primitive man, has also been driven to postulate infinity. Science has merely shattered a theology and, as Jesus constantly pointed out to the Pharisees, theology is not the same thing as religion.

Few tasks in history will be harder than the reconstruction of Christian theology in an age dominated by science among the educated and by industrialism among the masses. It will be a task calling for consummate religious genius. Yet it is well for us to remember that new symbols have been forged before, and more than once.

Jesus, followed by the apostles and early saints, performed this mighty service for the world of the Roman Empire and ultimately transformed it. When Jesus was born, the Roman Empire was as materialistic as is the United States today. Its learned philosophers were, if possible, more bumptiously ignorant of the spiritual needs of the masses than are modern scientists, taken as a class. There was the same growing weariness of spirit, the same intellectual snobbery and hand-washing on the part of the so-called intelligentsia, the same emphasis on efficiency and organization among the "practical" men, the same tendency to measure a man's worth in terms of social and national service.

There was even the same danger that "western" civilization might be overrun by the barbarian tribes.

But there is another, and a very laudable, aspect to our present situation which most of us, guilt-haunted as we are, never seem to consider. In our realization of what we have lost, we too frequently forget the enormous amount we have gained. If we on this continent have largely lost the capacity to be near to God, we have perhaps gained the capacity to be near to Jesus.

To me, who speak only as a layman, the stupendous achievement of the early Christian church consists in the link it contrived to forge between the conception of God and the conception of Jesus Christ. At the present time in North America the conception of Jesus—at least of Jesus, the Son of Man—has been so assimilated by the people that we have almost come to take that assimilation for granted.

If Jesus had not lived and taught, the boy with whom I had such an extraordinary discussion several years ago wou'd never have been the kind of person he was and still is. He is kindly, gentle, merciful, thoughtful of others, eager to help others, temperate, honorable and self-sacrificing. I think of that boy constantly whenever I hear my contemporaries talking about the younger generation.

Young men on this continent today are gentler and kindlier than they were when I was young, and when I was a boy we were gentler and kinder than boys were in my father's generation. Bullying is virtually extinct, except among the underprivileged in large cities and in backward areas like the southern states.

146

In adult life in North America there is much to be found with which Jesus would be pleased—more pleased than He could ever have been by the habits of men in the far more religious seventeenth century. People have become more considerate in their dealings with one another. They are more tolerant. They have come to feel a profound sense of responsibility toward the under-privileged.

The idea of charity on a vast national scale—which the United States has twice practised within a single generation—would have been unthinkable one hundred years ago. No European or Asiatic nation has ever shown charity in such proportions. We would do less than justice to the Protestant churches of North America if now, in the hour of their decline, we failed to acknowledge that Christ's example of merciful living has passed over into our habits, and we have largely the churches to thank for it.

The Jesus whom the Protestant churches of North America preached to their people was almost invariably a practical Jesus. In their puritanism many preachers made God appear like a vengeful monster, they denuded their services of beauty and art and even of good taste, yet they did succeed in making their people understand the sense of mercy which Jesus introduced into religion. It was seldom the mercy of the atonement—according to Calvin, redemption was only for the elect—but it was certainly the more homely mercy of the Jesus who healed the sick and pitied the poor, who turned the water into wine and performed the miracle of the loaves and fishes, who drove the money-lenders out of the temple and rebuked snobbery by the parable of the Good Samaritan.

This we should remember now, when thoughts of failure haunt us.

147

But we should also remember that the conception of the practical Jesus is only one aspect of the Christian religion, and perhaps not the most essential one. Our great need today is for a new vision of God, and already our most advanced thinkers—even some who a few years ago loudly trumpeted the glories of materialism—have at least recognized the truth that man does not live alone by bread and machinery.

It would be absurd, as well as insulting to our integrity as free-thinking human beings, to look for some master plan which would lead us to conversion. The journey of the whole people toward a new vision of God will not likely be much shorter or more direct than was the long and devious road which led them away from the old one.

History can strike quickly but it moves slowly. Three hundred and twenty-six years intervened between the birth of Jesus and the acceptance of Christianity by the ancient world as its official religion. Now and for many years, perhaps for centuries, a common cry of well-meaning men is likely to be that of the man in the Scriptures: "Help Thou mine unbelief!"

While this road is being traversed—perhaps I should say if the insanities of the national states leave anyone alive to traverse it—there is no need for us to feel guilty about our state of mind. There is no need for us, as individuals, to feel shamed by our spiritual incapacity. If millions lack the comfort of believing in the symbols of Christianity which helped our forefathers in their attempt to lead spiritual lives, we can at least do our best to live earthly lives in accordance with the ethics of Jesus Christ, as we search for a new way to express the idea of God.

9

A SECOND LOOK

Being misunderstood makes me uncomfortable, even when it brings me acclaim. In the past, whenever readers of one of my pieces have asked me to explain my meaning, I have replied that my words must stand up for themselves. This time, however, I have given in to the temptation to reply. I have written a postscript to the foregoing article, for inclusion here.

A SECOND LOOK

For weeks my mailbox has been crammed every day with letters, pamphlets and sermons sent from every section of Canada by enthusiastic adherents of various messiahs. Not only had I greatly underestimated the number of people who are searching sincerely for a new way of expressing the idea of God, I had also under-estimated the number of quacks, plagiarists, imposters, megalomaniacs and confused do-gooders who were eager to tell me that they had the answers which would settle all the problems of the age.

When the influx started I tried to read all the letters with an open mind because now and then I came upon one in which the obvious seriousness of the writer was genuinely moving. I even read the pamphlets and sermons for a while, until I discovered that in two respects they were nearly all alike: they showed a shame-less willingness to plagiarize misunderstood fragments of Mary Baker Eddy and an equally shameless tendency to mate these bits of pseudo-Christian Science with some of the better-known sayings of Dale Carnegie.

"Think about God," they all said in effect, "and in no time you will find yourself gaining friends, losing your ills and making money." It was a relief one morning to receive a missive from a staunch fundamentalist who said, "If God didn't save His own Son on the cross, what do you think He is going to do to you?"

Perhaps I would have been less surprised by this correspondence if I had read some of the recent best-sellers in both fiction and non-fiction, books which not only lower standards of taste and thought but reach new depths in their attempts to popularize religion. One of them presents the gospel story—the most nearly perfect work of literature in existence—in the threadbare narrative of a cheap thriller. Another turns it into modern journalese. Bringing the story of the apostles into what is considered updated language by giving them nicknames is hardly likely to increase one's respect for the kind of men they were, though it will, to be sure, sell books.

Emphatically, I did not have this sort of thing in mind when I wrote of the need to recreate orthodox theology to meet modern needs. It seems to me better to maintain an attitude such as that of William Jennings Bryan, who stated under oath that he believed even the misprints in the Bible, than to vulgarize and debase it to the level of an advertisement for patent medicine.

Many of the letters I received asked me to answer the questions I had posed. Had I been able to answer them I should have had no need to write on the subject. But I do believe that a supreme crisis exists in the lives of all of us at this time, and perhaps it cannot be stated too often what it is.

A chasm has always yawned between those who are capable of rational thought and those who are not. This chasm was formerly bridged by the Christian ritual. Today, among Protestants, that bridge has broken down. As the Rt. Reverend Irving S. Cooper stated the problem in a sermon—speaking of the insistence of the orthodox in presenting religion to a scientific age in childish and primitive terms—"these and many other Christian teachings are rapidly being pushed into their last resting-place, the minds of the ignorant."

It seems to me a tragic situation, after so many centuries of union, that the Greco-Christian civilization should split into its two original parts, rational humanism and uncritical faith, and that we should be asked to choose between them. There is no reason why the mystical approach to a vision of God—the approach followed by Jesus Himself—should be incompatible with modern scientific discoveries. Indeed, modern psychology has only corroborated the transcendent insight of Jesus into the workings of the human mind. There is, however, a reason why science and religion should *seem* incompatible to a modern man trained in the end-product of puritan education which we now see in operation on the North American continent. This is an educational system which has always insisted on the primacy of established facts and concrete results. It is inevitable that a man who approaches life in the spirit of an Edison should ultimately arrive at the conclusion that, while Jesus was undoubtedly remarkable for the time in which He lived, He is outmoded as an interpreter of the ways of God toward man.

Or take our modern atomic physicists. How does the

·educational system of today offset our knowledge that all of them, with telescopes and microscopes, with a profound knowledge of electricity, light-years and nuclear energy, possess more scientific information about God than Jesus gave any indication of knowing? Does not modern science acquaint the average North American with a thousand details about God's methods and achievements which the writers of the Gospels could not possibly have known?

The agnostic or semi-agnostic descendants of the Puritans—who were the first of the Protestants to dishonour the old mystical basis of Christianity—do not describe their position in the precise terms I have used here, but such assumptions underlie their conduct and their general attitude toward Christianity. When rebuked by the mystics for their lack of any real religion, they feel they can answer in Christ's own words: "By their fruits ye shall know them." Or, to phrase their position differently, since the United States and Canada— two countries which have always been dominated by the puritan tradition—have reached the highest peak of recorded human endeavour on a materialistic plane, they insist that the prosperity, and on the whole the justice, of the North American way of life proves its superiority.

So the end-product of puritanism has been enthroned, science unreconciled with religion, and by what seem to be logical steps we have been led into the solitude of a purposeless universe. This is what I believe to be the essence of the spiritual crisis we face. We are alone and we are purposeless.

Whether or not we can do anything about it is another question. I believe we can, if science will discard its traditional attitude of aloof irresponsibility and take definite steps toward the development of a genuine synthesis of knowledge. Orthodox science repudiates teleology—the basis of Aristotle's "common-sense philosophy" which asserts that every thought and every undertaking seems to aim at some purpose. It is convenient for scientists to act on the assumption that the universe is purposeless because such a premise releases their minds from preconceived ideas as well as from the tendency to shrink from new and startling knowledge which might upset an established system of thought. The scientist is an anarchist. He is trained into a state of readiness to overthrow any system, authority, prejudice or religion when his researches encourage him to do so. Toward nature he is usually humble; toward his fellow-man his arrogance is at times sublime.

In the face of such training, few scientists have made any motion toward a synthesizing of knowledge, and yet they are the only ones in our day who are capable of doing so with intelligence. To go one step further in such reasoning, it is only from a new synthesis of verified knowledge that any form of theology can develop which will satisfy the needs of a scientifically trained man.

Had Christ been born five centuries earlier, his teaching would never have reached the Gentiles, for it was St. Paul who took Christ beyond Judæa, and he could not have done so had his way not been paved by the great work of synthesis developed by Socrates, Plato, Aristotle, Epicurus, Zeno and Plotinus in the centuries immediately preceding the Christian era.

It is for science to formulate in intelligible terms the concepts of God-as-purpose and God-as-origin. If it fails to do so, modern man will lack religion in exact proportion to the extent of his education. Mystical interpretation of these concepts of God no longer touches the scientifically trained.

Nobody understood this essential truth more clearly than did St. Paul. When Jesus preached in Judæa He spoke to a semi-oriental people whose habit of thought was essentially mystical. When St. Paul preached to the Gentiles he addressed himself to men who had inherited a vast body of rational philosophy, to men acquainted with the scepticism of Pyrrho, the atomic theory of Democritus, the medical practice of Hippocrates, the precise engineering of the builders of the Roman aqueducts. The ultimate experience which St. Paul offered to this sophisticated world was a mystical one, but he based its validity on careful arguments drawn from the framework of philosophy which was the peculiar glory of the ancient Greeks. He argued with the Ephesians, the Thessalonians, the Corinthians, the Athenians and the Romans within their own frames of reference. He asked no one to believe blindly.

Yet it is only through mystical or poetic insight that man's ultimate experience—his relationship to the Universal Spirit—can be realized. Not all the exact knowledge in the world can substitute for the state of being which the wisdom of the centuries has affirmed to be the highest state to which the human spirit can rise.

The task of science is not to replace this state of mind by that of a laboratory detective; it is to provide conditions of thought in which such a state of mind can grow and rest. In other words, it must create a theology which seems reasonable to a scientifically trained man.

In the lonely hours of the night a nuclear physicist, dying of cancer and at the same time suffering from an oedipus complex, is not likely to find rest unto his soul by contemplating the traditional father-image of God,

10

THE TYRANNY OF THE SUNDAY SUIT

One of the worst handicaps under which a writer labours is his inability to make his words smile for him. When I gave this address to the Canadian Club in Toronto, somebody in the audience laughed with me during my warming-up remarks. A lot of other people laughed, too, and from that moment on we all had a fine time together. It was only the next day, when I read the newspaper reports of what I had said, that I sounded like a pretty cantankerous fellow.

The age of the stuffed shirt in Canada has passed its zenith, but we are left with the weight of its legacy. To my mind, the best thing to do with that legacy is to laugh it out of existence. It is too late for Canadians to enter the field of de-bunking in international letters; that period ended in 1939 and Canada had no part in it. But a good deal of de-bunking could still be salutary here at home. It will be a great day for Canada when one of our historians or biographers puts his hands on Lord Strathcona's beard and pulls it off. Nothing scandalous will be disclosed with the pulling, but a man who more than any other in Canada established the fashion of the stuffed shirt will become human, not a little ridiculous, and even possibly rather wonderful. The same goes for most of our famous men whom we still talk about in public with the solemnity of an obituary.

THE TYRANNY OF THE SUNDAY SUIT

I HAPPEN to believe that one of the most important goals in the life of the individual man is self-knowledge. I believe that the same goal is equally important for a nation. And I do not believe this self-knowledge can come, either to a man or to a country, as a gift from heaven. It is achieved only by long searching, continuous study, frankness, and a willingness to look on the bad as well as the good.

Whatever the start we may have made in Canada in recent years in our quest for self-knowledge, we have still a long way to go before we can claim to understand ourselves. Until we do, it is absurd to pity ourselves because we are not known to others.

All of us, whether we admit it nor not, are advanced or retarded by the mythology we invent or accept about ourselves. Mythology is fundamental to any society, and from the days of primitive man it has been inseparable from human life. A good myth is much more than a fairy tale. It is a symbol which dramatizes a popular point of view and gives an emotional content to daily experience. A mythology which is based on reality is one of the most valuable assets a people can possess. The symbol of Britannia as a sea-goddess has inspired Englishmen for centuries, not because Britannia was depicted as a beautiful woman, but because she symbolized the truth of a real situation: England's greatness, even her existence, dependent on her mastery of the sea.

When Britain was menaced by Napoleon, an English poet wrote:

> Britannia needs no bulwarks,
> No towers along the steep;
> Her march is o'er the mountain waves
> Her home is on the deep.

A century later, when another ballad singer sensed the imminence of Britain's decline, he turned to the same legend and invoked it for support:

> We sailed wherever ship could sail,
> We founded many a mighty state.
> Pray God our greatness may not fail
> Through craven fears of being great.

In the months following Dunkirk, Britain and her seamen once again pledged themselves to each other. When Roosevelt suggested that the Royal Navy be given haven in American waters in case of defeat, Churchill told him that if Britain were defeated there would be no Royal Navy, for Britain and her myth would go down together. This is what I would term a creative mythology. For a good many generations even Canadians living on the prairies have drawn sustenance from its shadow.

But our own most popular native symbol, which is represented by the red jacket of the Mounted Police, cannot possibly lead to a creative myth. I mean to say nothing derogatory against the finest police force in the world. I would like to point out, however, that only in a certain sense does the figure of the Mounted Policeman serve a sound symbolical purpose. He dramatizes our frontier, to be sure, but so few of us live there. For Canadians who live maturely, the Mounted Policeman as a symbol leads to a mythology which at best is of dubious emotional value. It can't help implying that the underlying impulse of our society is to punish anyone who steps out of line. It suggests that our principle is not to encourage, but to forbid. It suggests that we are prouder of the things we refrain from doing than of the things we do.

In making this protest I am aware that I am retelling an old story. I only wish it were such an old story that we could forget it. Too many manufacturers of Canadian products which are sold in the United States use Mounties on horseback in their advertisements; too many of our tourist folders, which at present constitute our most widely read native literature, continue to depict Canada in the light which their creators believe will most appeal to Americans—as a continuing frontier. The end-product is not so much the sense of disappointment Americans feel when they heed the invitation of the advertisements and find the country when they get here to be something else than they had expected; it is the bad effect it has on us. Unconsciously we tend to think of ourselves as interesting only in those aspects of our lives which Americans are led to consider of interest.

Not long ago I was lunching with one of the editors of a

widely read American monthly magazine. The purpose of the lunch on his part was to persuade me to write what he called a factual piece about Canada today. I found him in every respect a charming man, well informed generally, competent and friendly. He professed genuine fondness and respect for our country, but in everything he said about it, it was obvious that he considered French-speaking Canada to be a romantic backwater and most of English-speaking Canada an Arctic frontier.

Did I have anything in mind, he wanted to know, for a piece they could use? I made a number of suggestions, but at each one he frowned and shook his head. I tried him on something I considered tremendously important—the manner in which industry has shattered the traditional thought-pattern of French-Canada.

"No," he said, "that's not the kind of thing we're after. Look here—will you give us something on husky dogs?"

He was so serious I hadn't the heart to laugh in his face. "I've never lived in the Arctic," I said.

"Well, what about this? Give me a piece on a trapper. A loveable rogue."

I told him the only trapper I had ever met was an old reprobate who trapped lobsters on the shore of one of the less thickly inhabited counties of Nova Scotia whenever his credit ran out with the bootlegger. But that wasn't what he wanted either. They'd done something fairly recently on lobster fishermen in Maine.

"What about a Mountie?" said the editor.

It was the inevitable question and with it I gave up. Toward the end of the luncheon, when one further topic was broached—bears, could I do something on bears?—I tried to explain that the most significant stories to be found in Canada today must come out of the cities and towns. The greatest story in modern Canada would be our version—an individually different version—of the greatest story in the world at the present time. It would be based on the ferment brewing in the minds of young people as they tried to discover a new purpose, both for themselves and for their country, in a world where most of their inherited values and attitudes had been shattered. Why, I said to my host, should not the lives of truly representative Canadians be more interesting than picturesque traders on the fringes?

"You're all wrong," he said. "I know what Americans want to read. A few years ago we ran a piece about Mackenzie King and it was a flop. Between ourselves, people thought it was dull. I know he's able—we could use a few men like him down in Washington—but if your Prime Minister is like that, people think everybody else up here is like that, too. After all, you've kept him in office for more than twenty years. I've got to find somebody who will give me something on husky dogs."

The fault in his thinking, I submit, was not his but ours. For years we have permitted a dynasty of dullness to control our manners, to speak for us in public, to reduce all the bright colours in our spectrum to a drab and blameless grey. We put red coats on our Mounted Police, but stuffed shirts on our official spokesmen. Far too many of our leaders, in business as well as in politics, display an almost psychopathic conviction that the less they dramatize reality, the less likely it is that reality will rise up and bite them. Again and again they congratulate themselves on what a well-behaved country Canada is. Again and again they suggest—with subtlety but with devastating effect—that the man who speaks out in a clear voice is unsound.

Perhaps there is something to be said for any point of view which succeeds in securing its objective, even if that objective is merely to retain political power as long as possible. For what difference does it make, our architects of dullness might say, whether we are coherent or not? At least we are protected against the kind of vulgar ribaldry American politicians have to put up with from their newspapers. There are advantages in being dull. One of our most able diplomats has insisted to me that if Canada were really known abroad, foreigners would become envious of her. There are also advantages in being cautious. What difference does it make whether we think of our lives as a great adventure? Adventurous people always get into trouble. Is it not a fact that if Canada had produced a flamboyant character like Winston Churchill, Ottawa would have cut him down to size and sent him back to his native province where he might, with luck, have become a provincial premier or the mayor of a disgruntled town? Let no one make a mistake, our politicians of the past generation knew what they were doing. They have let us know in a hundred subtle ways that there is no room in Canadian public life for anyone who is unsound enough to utter a principle so clearly that everyone can understand it.

Such a doctrine of public behaviour, I insist, is outmoded. During a brief interlude in our history, following the conscription crisis of 1917, there was some excuse for this kind of caution, but there is none now. Perpetual caution can succeed only in a second-rate society. Moreover, those who consider security to be man's chief end—whether the security be economic or mental—must inevitably lose the very security they seek, for a people bereft of a challenge will soon atrophy.

More important than anything else, however, is the effect of such an apotheosis of dullness on the youth of the country. Young people are dramatic by nature.

The natural challenges of life are a stimulus to them. They all know—as someone once wrote in a letter to *Time*—that "emotional buoyancy and mental health do not arise from a cautious avoidance of conflict, but from the ability of the personality to maintain a balance between dangerous drives of varying intensity."

Endless reams are still being written about the magnet below the border which sucks at our youth as though they were so many iron filings to be lured away from the austere virtues of the native scene by the promise of larger salaries and greater material benefits. Such reasoning is fallacious. It is based on the refusal to face reality lest reality turn and bite hard. Young Canadians are moving down to the United States to live and work because they like it better there. They have become so fed up with the emotional caution of their elders that they are leaving Canada in droves to live in a country which has never been afraid to dramatize herself, never afraid to be vulgar in its process of trying to achieve coherence. With all the mistakes she makes, the United States remains unafraid of making them, and therein lies the excitement young people feel in the life of that country.

Do not mistake the point I am trying to make. If I thought Canada really were a dull country, I would not be here today. I happen to be one of those Canadians who once tried to live in the United States and returned because I liked it better at home. The individual Canadian, with a few notable exceptions, is not a dull person at all. He is not—again with a few notable exceptions which have taken their place in the public mind as typical Canadians—a stuffed shirt. On the contrary, he is one of the most complex, one of the most intricately adjusted, one of the most civilized, one of the most fascinating species of the human race now in existence. Under his matter-of-fact surface he is a creature of astonishing variety, as foreigners invariably point out when they know him well. The trouble with Canada is not the individual as such. It is the devastating fact that for too long we have been led to believe, by the examples held before us, that we must talk and behave in public as though we were entirely different men from the individuals we know ourselves to be.

As long as we accept this Canadian principle which insists that in public we must always wear a Sunday suit and a stiff white collar, just so long will Canada remain a country in which no one else in the world is especially interested. And as long as she appears to be dull, just so long will thousands of our best young brains take their talents out of Canada for what seems to be a richer life in the United States.

What I am going to say now may sound like a contradiction to everything that has gone before, but I assure you it is not. I have said that the young people of Canada are going south in droves because the United States seems more exciting than the Dominion. There are others, the not-so-young, who are going to the United States against their wills. They are going down in order to advance in their professions, or merely to stay in them and at the same time keep alive. These men, we might easily say, are leaving for purely economic reasons. But if we look far enough, we can see that the rule of dullness has driven them south, too.

There is no point in any of us bemoaning the fact that we are a poor country in comparison to the United States. We still have the second highest living-standard in the world, and we still have plenty of money to spend, publicly and privately, for the enrichment of life in this country. Our ailment is the state of mind which so consistently prevents the money from being spent where it can do the greatest good. Many of our public men these days tell us that the most grievous threat to our national future—short of an atomic war—lies in the emigration of our best talent. They use glibly the word "duty" every time they urge their sons to stay at home, and they have been doing this ever since I can remember. What do they think Canada is—a mission-field? Do Americans and Englishmen, do Swedes and the Swiss, feel it necessary to keep their sons in their native lands by appealing to their sense of duty? On the contrary, they take it for granted that the only national resources for which too much can never be paid are brains and talent.

Are Canadian institutions paying the most they possibly can to keep our best brains at home? Business enterprises may be doing so; I am too ignorant of most fields of manufacture and merchandise in Canada to know whether they are or not. But in the fields where the most disastrous emigration of our best talents occurs, Canadian institutions most emphatically are *not* paying anything close to the sums they would if they had the imagination to realize what their cautious counting of pennies is costing both them and the nation.

The most important profession in this or any other country is the teaching profession. It is in the schools and colleges that men are inspired or dispirited, that the foundations of their adult points of view are laid. It is in the schools particularly that we all develop the basic emotional relationships toward society which last for the rest of our lives. It is in the schools that a nation comes to know itself.

In Canada, how much are the men and women paid

upon whom we rely to maintain the schools and perform these functions?

Six years ago, when I was asked by the Canadian Broadcasting Corporation to write a script for a broadcast on the state of education in Canada, I realized the moment I saw the salary scales that to talk about curriculums, about the desirability of this or that teaching method, would be a hypocritical waste of time. To a man dying of thirst in the desert, all the delights of civilization pale in comparison with a single mug of water. There was only one aspect of the situation to discuss, and that was money. Not only was the average wage paid to a school teacher in Canada disgracefully below the level of wages paid to a teacher in Great Britain; it was less than that paid to unskilled, non-unionized labour in the poorest of our own provinces.

The response to this broadcast, I have since learned, was similar to the response which is invariably made to any exposure of the plight of teachers in Canada. Nineteen Canadians out of twenty probably agreed with my insistence that no country is better than its schools, no schools better than its staffs, and no staffs likely to be first-rate if they are paid barely enough to keep alive. But those who agreed with me either told me privately it was a shame about the teachers or kept a decorous silence. And into the void of that silence jumped the usual oafs who only too often, and always by default, contrive to appear as spokesmen for our communities. One man wrote that it was wiser to let sleeping dogs lie. Another wrote that it would be wicked to increase the teachers' salaries; if you did, you would attract into the profession undesirable persons whose chief motive would be gain. Several said, "The teachers are being paid just what they got when I went to school, and if they were good enough for me, they're good enough for my children." One man wrote, "The teacher in our village is getting $450 a year, and that's twice what she's worth. Forty years ago you could get a teacher for $150."

So much for elementary education in Canada. What of our universities?

I am old enough to remember the day when we had reason to be proud of them. Compared to those of the United States, they were on the whole superior to any but a few institutions like Harvard and Yale. I would not like to argue rashly for their superiority now. How could I, when some of them are paying their professors on a salary scale that is virtually the same as it was when salaries were set in the last century? No wonder our universities were so good fifty years ago; a four-thousand-dollar chair in 1900 could attract the kind of men Harvard can attract now with a twelve-thousand-dollar chair. We're beginning to take for granted the lamentations heard in our universities because the geniuses and Nobel Prize winners who *once* graced their faculties now work in the United States, or in Brazil, or even in Australia. Unfortunately it takes imagination to understand the effect a truly creative teacher will have on a generation of students.

So much for higher education in Canada.

Radio has been, from its beginning, a fertile field for the maturing of young talent in Canada. We all know names of young men who have helped raise it to the high standards we have come to take for granted in our best native programmes. One of them I know rather better than some of the others. You would know him, too, if I mentioned his name. For ten years he worked exceedingly hard as a radio playwright. No man can put in more than three hundred and sixty-five days every year.

But even after ten years and continuous successes on the air, he was forced to add up his accounts, for he was still living from hand to mouth. He had a wife and children, but no savings. He is a rather shy young person, and it took courage to ask the radio companies to pay him what he considered a worthy price for his scripts. But he received the old worn-out answers: Canada is a poor country. If you think you can do better, go to the States. Today he has his own private office in Rockefeller Centre, and his yearly earnings are five times what they were here. It's a pity, because he still prefers to live in Canada, and a year ago he would have settled for less than double what he was earning then.

Granted that private radio companies in Canada must operate on a scale much lower than that of the great American networks; but granted also that we have a government-operated radio corporation which the taxpayers underwrite. The least it can do is to subsidize talent, Canadian talent. Its avowed purpose is to protect and promote Canadian culture. The fees for talent would amount only to a small fraction of the cost involved in the maintenance of the industry as a whole. One good native playwright, working on our radio, would be worth more to this country than a hundred tons of government pamphlets, or a hundred miles of useless road built into the bush before a general election.

For many years the government of Finland, a country far less wealthy than Canada, has paid a pension to Jan Sibelius to enable him to continue composing music. At no time have his symphonies earned, in actual cash, a fraction of the cost of his pension, but the Finns did not measure the value of Sibelius by the standards of the market-place. They were mature enough to understand that they needed him and that he needed them.

The bread the Finns cast upon the waters returned to them, augmented a thousand times, in 1939, when Russia attacked their country. Soldiers in the Mannerheim Line and on ski patrols knew that in England and America hundreds of thousands of people were emotionally concerned with their fate. They knew that Englishmen and Americans were listening to *Finlandia*, *Valse Triste* and the symphonies played over and over again on the radio networks. The man Sibelius, his music and his country were fused into a sense of gratitude in the minds of powerful and distant nations, and though the Finns fought bravely, and were in any case respected, it was largely owing to Sibelius that their national survival became a matter of such emotional importance to the western world. Their determination to make it possible for Sibelius to continue living in his native land was more than a gesture to culture; it was an attitude of wise self-interest. The Finns well understood that while a nation may become known to strangers because of its politicians and its crimes, it is only through its arts that it can become loved.

While I was preparing this address, I broke off work to walk on the terrace on the roof of my apartment building in Montreal. It was nine-thirty in the evening. Cars were streaming down the slope of Côte des Neiges in a steady cascade. Less than a mile away, on a lower level, the lights in the Sun Life Building showed that cleaners were at work in the empty offices. Across the St. Lawrence an undulating bracelet of light marked the line of the farther shore. The smoke shrouding the acres of slums near the left bank of the river glowed and smouldered in the lights striking through it. Nearer, more intimate lights were all around me in hundreds of windows in apartment buildings where families were resting, listening to the radio, reading books and newspapers, talking over the events of the day. Within a radius of half a mile husbands were loving their wives or quarrelling with them, broken men were staring at the beer-spills on tavern tables, doctors were operating in the hospitals, brave men and women were fighting for their lives under oxygen tents, babies were being born. A little farther to the east, in one of the laboratories at McGill, a few late-working scientists were slowly edging their way a little nearer to new truths. Here, almost within the sound of a shout, was a vast congeries of private lives which every day spill over into the public life of the country. Close-packed around them were more than a million memories throbbing with the recollections of a trillion private experiences. Despair entered one room as hope entered the room below it, one man brooded on how to destroy an opponent while another searched for means of recovering a lost friend. It was all familiar, yet it was all different; it had all happened countless times before, yet each time any one of these things happens it seems to be new.

Here was Canada, only a small part of it, but here it was. It had only to know itself.